ANKANA

Love is a process, Not a moment

A Novel By

ANUPAM CHATTERJEE

With Blessings from my parents and family

Dedicated to

The love stories around me

INTRODUCTION

Men can be segregated in five behaviors when it comes to a love story around them.

The first one is ready to give up his identity to be in a relationship, to make her happy. He comes out someone who is scared of his lady, but frankly he is going that extra step to make the relationship work.

The second one is someone who has no clue how a love story works. He is in for a lifelong friend and who doesn't want to grow up. It is the lady who makes this story click.

The third one is someone who leaves it on time. He doesn't know how to start a love story, what to do when in one, and what to expect from his love. He is the eternal bachelor, who is happy seeing his friends having a love story.

The forth one is the committed type. He accepts that the love story comes with its own joy and pain, and he is matured to be happy being in a relationship. He understands his lady and loves her completely for what she is. He is stable and everyone looks up to him.

The fifth one is the commitment phobic. He is also the one who goes in and out of multiple relationships. He knows how to start a love story but doesn't know how to sustain a love story.

This story is about the love story of the fifth one and these other four male friends of his. A story about his desire to have his last everlasting final relationship.

INDEX

1 --- The Gang Up

2 --- Marriage Bug Bites

3 --- Mean at Work

4 --- Joker Gets Cinderella

5 --- It does get Serious

6 --- I flow with the wind

7 ---Out of quicksand

8 --- I did try

9 --- Armaan's roller coaster ride

10 --- Finally we meet

11 --- Series of Firsts

12 --- The Love Grows

13 ---The cracks in the foundation

14 --- Anger

15 --- The Shit-Hole

16 --- The Self Exploration

The Gang-up

It was Sunday morning. I was sitting outside my balcony facing the sea, reading the morning newspaper over a cup of tea. The government had again passed a bill to emphasize and provide better working conditions to the poorer section of the society. The economic condition of the country had been upbeat for quite some time and it looked promising. The national cricket team had won another tournament and, had again cemented their position as the best side in all forms of the game. The critic section was empty and there was no burning issue in the country. A light cool breeze was flowing from south. It was the ideal weather to go out for a long drive.

I folded the newspaper, and walked towards my bed room. Tiger, my Golden Retriever who was all this time sitting by my side looking at the sea swiftly followed my lead. I quickly changed into khaki shorts and a white t-shirt and walked to my basement garage. The elegant white Audi A8 was standing next to the muscular black BMW X6. But the weather outside was too good to be enjoyed. Hence I preferred my silver Jaguar XK convertible. Tiger jumped onto the navigator seat. We took over to the road by the sea shore lined with coconut trees. Tiger sat with his head over the windscreen enjoying the wind on his face. His light brown skin was shining like gold in the morning sun. We stopped at my hotel for a quick breakfast.

The computer whiz kid millionaire Tenfrey Wilson had been visiting India with his girlfriend and had checked into my hotel the previous night. The young couple was having breakfast in the wooden balcony by the pool side. I walked over to him to confirm if his stay was luxurious and up to his liking. He spoke highly with great appreciation of my country and my fellow citizens. We spoke briefly before I took his leave and walked towards my car. Tiger was busy playing with the guest kids in the garden area. I whistled for him and he came running and jumped on to his seat.

Next we took on the hilly road and stopped by my coffee estate. The moment I stopped the car, he jumped off and went barking towards the bush. He loves to run around the estate. My phone rang and took up the call. It was my mother.

"Its eleven in the morning and you are still sleeping. What are you doing with your life? When will you grow up?" she said.

For a few seconds I could not gather myself, but soon I realized I was dreaming in my deep sleep. I found my way outside the blanket, only to find that I had been sleeping over a pile of washed clothes on the other side of my bed. I turned over and fell on the ground by the bed. I straightened myself and sat over and searched for my phone which had slipped off my arm while I was coming to my senses. My mother was still speaking something. I cut her off "*Maa*, I will call you in five minutes. Atleast let me get fresh", and I hanged the call.

I walked over to the bathroom to brush my teeth, only to realize that I was out of toothpaste and it had been four days I had promised myself to buy a new tube. I have been in a habit of conveniently forgetting these basic survival groceries during the week. I took a note mentally for going down to the grocery store that very day. I washed my face and gargled with the cold tap water. I put some water in my palms and rubbed the back of my neck. It was refreshing and I came to my complete senses. My head was heavy and I was having a terrible pain on the right side of the head. While taking a leak I remembered that last night we friends were drinking over a bollywood movie. With the sudden realization, I peeked over to the hall. Piyush was sleeping on the floor with an empty bottle in his hand, and Armaan hanging over the couch with his legs spread across the table, clearly defying all laws of Physics. Potato chips were scattered all around the floor, and none of them retained their original shape or texture. The lights were still on. Last night was slowly coming back to me.

We all had gone for an IPL match in the Chinnaswamy stadium. On our way back we decided to stay over at my place and watch some good movie. We bought liquor and chips from the neighborhood super market and ordered for pizza on phone. After scanning the channels on the TV, we settled for an Aamir's movie as it had got good reviews and none of us had watched it. It was all going well before Arpit puked, and Armaan had a realization that we had been drinking lot and had a sudden change of heart. He wanted to watch the James bond movie which was due to start late in the night, and after sobering up a bit settled on the couch to watch the movie. Piyush had drifted into his own world of ecstasy. He was singing romantic songs to the bottle and at short intervals drinking directly from it. It was not long before he dozed off. I had offered Arpit lemon wedges and black coffee, but he had quietly declined it for his home remedy of putting his head below a tap of cold running water. I myself was feeling sleepy so I had walked over to my bed and fallen asleep instantly. Arpit had assured me that he will come to sleep on the other side of bed after drying off his head. But presently he was nowhere to be found.

My brains were working like a Bollywood detective tracing back one step a time to

uncover previous night's mystery. I walked back to my bedroom. I remembered that I had offered him a towel to dry off his head in the night. I could find the same towel on floor by the bed, but not Arpit. I searched him in the huge pile of cloths on my bed, but he was not there. The only other room in my small apartment was the kitchen, so I rushed to check him there. He was indeed there in a deep sleep sitting on the floor with his back firmly by the wall. When I tried to wake him up, he did with a sudden jolt and stood up. He looked at me with blank eyes as if trying to remember my name. As a robot his hands slowly moved up to rub his eyes. Suddenly he pushed me aside, got hold of a sauce pan kept by the burner and while filling water in it, he spoke

"What time is it? I have a lunch with Neha. She will kill me if I am late or if she finds me I had been drinking all night. I had told you all not to make such a plan. You know she will kill me"

I got pissed off and said "Wo!! Wo!! Wo!! Don't put this on us. You were equally involved in the plan. And what happens between you and Neha is none of our business"

He looked confused and was not even listening to me. He was searching for the coffee powder and muttering "she will kill me for this". I held him square by his forearms and gave him a sudden jerk and slapped him on his face. He came to his senses. Once I knew I had his attention, I said, "Its still ten past eleven. You have lot of time. Take a cup of coffee, take a head bath with cold water, catch an auto, go to your home, change your dress, and call Neha only after that".

"But what about my alcohol breath?" he protested

"Brush your teeth and have a full pack of mouth fresheners"

"But she will make out that I was drinking last night by my walk"

"Tell her that you overslept and when you woke up your legs have a bad pain, may be because you went for a Jog late last night with me"

"Yeah that will be a good excuse" he said "thanks for the idea *yaar*. I just hope she doesn't find out"

I did not know whether it was my irritation or sympathy for him, but I blurted out "Why are you always scared of her?"

He took a long breath and replied "because she is my fiancé and you will realize this only when you are in such a relationship"

I had no answer to this and hence I turned away from him to wake up Armaan.

Over the next hour everyone had black coffee, and after coming back to senses everyone realized they had some pending plans and they left. I prepared myself another cup of coffee and went to the terrace and called up my mother

"Yes *maa*, tell me."

"you took so long to call back"

"oh nothing. Few friends had stayed over. They all woke up when I did. Now they all left and hence I called up now so that we can talk freely"

"Which all friends? Why had they stayed over?" I could sense concern and inquisitiveness in her voice

"Arpit, Piyush and Armaan. We all had been to the cricket match yesterday. On our way back we planned to watch over a movie at my place. By the time movie ended it was quite late and hence they all stayed over" I preferred not to mention the drinking part.

"How many times I have told you not to hang around that Piyush. He is into all bad habits and he pulls you all also into them. And I could never understand that Armaan. He is always so quiet, as if hiding something from everyone. Arpit is a good sensible boy. You should stay with him. His marriage is also in a few months. He is so sensible. Why don't you learn something from him?" Since we all were childhood friends, and families living close to each other, my mother knew everything about them. Because of this fact, I always had to be completely aware of what I speak of them. I should not speak anything more and nothing less.

"Hmmm. So why had you called?" I tried to change the topic

"Because you do not call for weeks and being a mother I worry about you. You live all by yourself so far away from your home land, and that too with very limited sane friends" I could sense my mother turning around to get back to Arpit's topic. I knew if I try to act smart, my mother will make sure to discuss only that topic till either of us got irritated.

"No *maa*, you know whole week I am so busy with office. I don't get time. But I call on Sunday's na."

"That is why I say get married. You will get home on time, have home cooked food and will have ample time to call your old parents as well", and I knew why she had called. She continued "See Arpit. He is getting married to Neha. Both are so

sensible and are of same caste. Neha is two years younger also to him. Such a perfect pair they make." I wanted to tell how scared Arpit is of Neha. But I held myself back, because I knew my mention would become a hot colony gossip back home, and it could land Arpit and Neha and their families in a very complex situation.

"Yeah. That is destiny *maa*. Things happen when it has to happen."

"Actually when some things have to happen, they are made to happen" she replied in protest and continued "it is time now, and you should get married. I have already seen a perfect girl for you, the daughter of the neighbors of your *mamaji* who lives in Indore. Her name is Disha and she is a sangeet visharad and very polite. She will make your home happy."

Here I haven't made up my mind to get married at first place, I even haven't thought about what kind of girl I would like to get married to, and my mother has already decided who will be good for me. And how does someone good at singing guarantee that she will keep the home happy.

"*Maa,* if I remember correctly, last time when we visited *mamaji,* around fifteen years back she was just a six or seven years old girl. How do you know she will be perfect for me? And have you even seen her latest photograph?" I replied in a protest, but trying to sound as calm as possible. My coffee was also over.

"See even you remember that girl from so long ago" I was caught in my own words

"That's because she was the only kid in the colony of my age and for complete month of our stay I had to play with her toys only" I tried to clarify things.

"Your *mamaji* has suggested her name and has spoken highly of her. And I am convinced with his choice." She replied with utmost confidence and the calmness of when the decision has been made. I immediately knew this topic has to be ended now and has to be avoided as much as possible. And I knew just the correct solution for all this

"Maa, I haven't had breakfast also, and I am very hungry. I am planning to directly go for lunch now. We will talk later"

"See this is why I say marriage is so necessary. Life will fall in a schedule and your health will improve. Anyways you go for your lunch. Where do you plan to eat?"

"I will go to the Bengali restaurant and have *rui doi mach, shukto, aloo postu aar bhath*". I knew I have played the trump card perfectly, and the devil inside me was smiling while he relaxed himself in a *hookah* bar.

"*Bhalo.* Go have food."

Marriage Bug bites

I went back to my bathroom and took a long shower. The whole time I was thinking about the words of my mother. Was it really an age to get married and settle down! Would I be able to handle all the responsibilities! What kind of girl will I get married to! Will it be better to invest a few more years on career before taking this decision! What will the girl I get married to think about me and expect out of me! There were so many questions and doubts popping up in my head.

I put over my black jeans and navy blue t-shirt and locked my door behind me. On the ground floor, there was a common parking for the complete building. There was no assigned parking slot for anyone and everyone parked where they wished to. My Yamaha bike was parked by the east wall of the building and a car was parked diagonally across it, blocking the exit way. On closely looking I saw a few lap cushions on the back seat and also by the rear glass. The rear seat was covered with what looked like a miniature velvet couch cover. The front dashboard had a small doll depicting a girl and boy doing a salsa. A couple of small hearts were hanging by the neck of the rear view mirror. These were enough clues for me to figure out that the car belonged to the newly married couple who looked immensely in love, the Sharmas who stay on the first floor. I was getting late for my lunch and was really hungry. So I ran up to the first floor and knocked on Sharma's door. I could hear some mumbles from within the house, which became louder and louder till the door opened, and turned into a pin drop silence. Navin Sharma stood there looking blankly on my face, as if trying to recollect my existence. I cut his thoughts off saying, "I believe your car is parked in front of my bike blocking its path. If you could back it up a little I could take it out."

"Oh sure", came a prompt reply with a shy smile. He must have figured it out that I was the guy living on the third floor who rides the bike and who has wished him a morning or evening from under his helmet on previous several occasions. He went inside to fetch his car keys. With the door left ajar I couldn't stop overhearing the couple's quarrel.

The wife was saying, "you always have time to move your car up and down in the parking lot, but you never have time for me"

"there is a neighbor standing on the door. What will he think" protested the husband

"let him also know how insensitive you are to your wife and to your responsibilities"

"give me five minutes. I will come back and will find a solution"

"that is what you always promise to do and come back and get engrossed in computer or TV. You never have time for me"

Navin came out with a shy smile on his face and with a comment "well now I am married" as his defense. I gave back a smile. How could I tell him that what I heard was one of the scariest thoughts I have been deliberating over the past couple of months. I preferred to keep my thoughts to myself. A few minutes later I started my bike and waved thanks to Navin and off I went towards the Bengali restaurant. I was driving very slow and was lost in my thoughts. A sudden long honk by a big lorry brought me back to my awareness of the surroundings. I tried to focus on road till I reached my destination.

I was greeted by the familiar grin of Khota in the restaurant. My usual spot was occupied, so I walked up to the end of the large hall of the restaurant and took a seat by the corner table. Khota came running towards me to take my order. Since I was so regular to this place, even the waiters knew I know the menu by heart. I placed my order "*Rui doi mach, shukto, aloo postu, bhaat* and chilled *mishti doi* at the end. But first quickly bring me a glass of cold water". And he was gone into the kitchen. I could see lot of new faces and a few familiar ones. There was a gang of girls sitting somewhat in the middle of the hall looking towards me and smiling. As any other bachelor, I felt the sudden rush of confidence boost inside me. My thoughts went back to my previous relations when my girlfriends used to appreciate my looks and slim physique. Those thoughts brought a smile across my face. But slowly I realized the words of Shreyasi when we were breaking off. In the heated conversation she had told how abnormal I look with my thin physique and a big head with long grass like hairs all over it. The experience had taught me that the bitter truth is told only when spoken in anger, and hence I had the actual picture of my looks flashing across my head. I knew something had to be wrong for the girls to smile at me from across the table. I rushed to the washroom to have a look at me in the mirror. And it turned out that I had forgotten to comb my hairs after the bath. My head was looking like a barren land with a bunch of shrubs grown at few selected places among the grass. I could now place the blank look of Navin earlier in the day and the smile from the girls. I used my bare hands to comb my hair and put them in some decent formation before heading out back for my table. As I sat down I gave an assuring smile back at the girls, who by now were busy eating their share of *hilsa* and rice.

I had never been so observant of the restaurant customers, but today my thoughts

were somewhat different. I was observing every hungry soul there, one at a time. To my surprise more than half of the tables were occupied by couples, some married, some still exploring their options. But not all couples behaved similarly. Couples with kids were busy overlooking the younger ones while they ate fish. Neither of them were even looking at their spouse. Other married couples ate quietly focusing on their plates, once in a while pitching in with some short comments. The unmarried couples were the ones who looked hopelessly in love. The food on their table was getting less priority than the eyes of the partner. The group of bachelors sitting in the rest of the tables looked hungry and they were enjoying each other's company. Khota came with my order and an added bowl of *aamer chatney*. He declared that on the house. I did not want to make any conclusions of my recently attained observational powers, so I just preferred to give love to my hungry stomach.

Once done I washed my hands and walked towards the counter where Chottun was watching the small TV kept under his counter table. He looked up from the TV at me, and said

"That will be hundred and fifty rupees *Daksh da*."

While I fetched for cash in my wallet, he continued "Don't mind *Daksh da*, but should I tell you one thing. You were the only one here eating alone. Earlier you used to come with *Shubho da,* but after his marriage you come alone. I feel bad for you. Why don't you also get married! Even we would like to see you come here with *Boudi*".

Khota also pitched in "Yes *Daksh Da*, get married"

I looked at them with a little forced smile on my lips and handed the exact cash to Chottun, took some fennel and sugar kept in the bowls on the counter and walked out. Somehow I was not able to appreciate the whole marriage topic. But it was very clear that I needed some thinking on this topic.

On my way home I stopped at the local supermarket near my home. I had to pick up toothpaste. But I thought of giving a walk through all the aisles just in case I remember something else that was needed at home. On my way through the aisles I crisscrossed many females, and all I could think of was whether a similar girl will be perfect for me. I was feeling ashamed of myself while these thoughts kept popping in my head but I had no control on my mind, which kept coming back to the marriage topic. I had to control my thoughts so I gave a call to Shubho as soon as I was back home. He had been my best friend over all these years and was the most sensible person I knew on this topic.

"Hey Daksh, how are you. Long time man" said the familiar voice

"I am fine. You only have got busy post marriage and don't have time for your old friends" I counter replied him.

"Marriage does come with lot of responsibilities, and a new person in your life. It takes lot of effort and time to find the proper comfort zone for peaceful life"

"You sound even more matured after your marriage" I tried to set a softer tone for our conversation as I wanted to be in my comfort zone while I could get a few answers

"Ha ha. You can call it maturity, I will call it evil reality" he continued "and may I know what reminded you of your old friend at a Sunday evening which the younger Daksh would have preferred for some crazy date"

"That was long time back. I think my share of relationships is done. I just cannot be someone else just to impress a girl. I have left those times long behind me"

"Hmmm!! Sounds like you have befriended your inner self. That's a nice development."

"Ha ha" I smiled and continued "I actually wanted to discuss a few things with you. Hope Ruchi *boudi* won't mind"

"And why should she mind?"

"Because I have seen that after marriage men have to take permissions from their wives. Most of my friends have to, and even Arpit has to"

He laughed aloud and replied "That is because the balance of the house is not proper. In our case it is perfectly balanced. If you want I will get her also in the call"

"If you don't mind I would like to discuss to a friend. Man to man"

"And so I thought about my newly converted shy friend" he spoke with a giggle. He continued in a sincere tone "tell me what is the issue"

"My parents feel that I should get married, but I am not quite sure. I am confused" I said

"What are you confused about"

"I am not quite sure. The word marriage itself is sounding scary and I do not know how to respond and how to proceed ahead"

"Why do you think marriage is scary?" he asked

"I see all my friends have lost their freedom after they got married. They do not have time for friends. They are always in a tensed or irritated. It's scary."

"See I do not know how and from where you have picked up this perception. But marriage is an age old system of civilized society which has been followed for generations after generations for the benefit of mankind. It is the same bond which your parents are in. It is the nature's law that every human is half and the spouse completes the other half, and together they make a complete system"

"Definitions are fine, but don't you think these talks suit well for the previous generations. For our generation these logics are quite obstinate"

"Every generation thinks the same way Daksh. Even I can guarantee your father's generation thought the same way about your grandfather's generation. But that does not mean definition of marriage changes"

"But you did not answer my doubts" I protested

"Marriage is a process in which you bond to a person who promises to be with you in all good and bad, one who is the only friend when you are old and lonely. A time comes when your friends are busy with their own world, when they do not find time like the younger days, and in those times you find your spouse by your side. The sooner you accept this fact, the more fun this relationship will be"

"But why the fights? Why the tension among spouses?" I protested

"Marriage is a relationship where both partners are equal. Think of a scenario in real life when someone befriends you and tries to dominate you. Or one who befriends you and expects to follow you at every step. In either situation you will feel irritated. Isn't it?"

"Yes I suppose I will"

"And your irritation can grow to anger, to which the new friend may object to"

"Yes I suppose so"

"Now consider this newly befriended person as your wife. Even from her side the same scenario applies"

"Yes I agree to this"

"But being equal is a theoretical term. In practical life, such a system is not

possible. On situation to situation either person takes up the dominating and the submissive qualities. That is required in smooth functioning of the household. But in situations where both try to be dominating or being submissive, the tension arises"

"That is what I am saying. It cannot be avoided" I emphasized again on my thought process

"This understanding has to be built between the partners on their own. No one else can walk in to their relationship and define the scenarios and responsibilities. Remember a clap requires two hands my dear. If you are matured enough and pull yourself to reciprocate your partner, you can maintain peace"

"But why should I only have to"

"Actually both of you have to. But someone has to take the initiative. You both can't sit waiting for the other one to take the initiative. If you take the initiative, she will realize one day and she will appreciate your efforts and one day she will also start. But as a matter of fact, being a female she is created to initiate this. She will put in her efforts. The onus will be on you to be a man and identify such scenarios and appreciate her effort and also reciprocate her actions from your side"

"I understand all these, but still fights will happen"

"If you mean by the difference of opinions, yes that will always happen. Every human has a right to have an opinion. And a man should respect others opinion."

"But as friends when we have different opinions we don't fight. But couples do"

"that's because as friends we go back to our individual lives after the difference of opinion. But in a marriage a couple has to come back to each other only and live with the difference of opinion" he replied in a calm voice

"You sound like there is no way out of marriage and that making it work all depends on us"

"Is there a way out of marriage Daksh?"

"I wish to find one"

"That is up to you. No one can force marriage on you. But if proper efforts are put, it is a beautiful relationship" he continued "I know you have issues and differences with people and hence you prefer not to have a room partner. But your spouse happens to be your permanent room partner. The day you realize this fact and mature enough to appreciate this, your life will do wonders"

"But you know I have been in so many relationships. And none of them have succeeded. To show myself as the man in front of friends, I can count multiple issues on which the girl failed to live up to my expectations. But the fact is I end up screwing every relation. I am just not a relationship kind of guy"

"I have never told you upfront, but I always knew you were getting into relationships because of mere attractions. But the fact has been that you backed out of every relationship the instant you saw any trouble. Relationships are about compromises. With maturity the person makes more compromises."

"But why should I compromise. Why not her"

"You never know. She may have made compromises but you would have not noticed it."

"And how can you say so"

"I am just speculating. She may have or she may have not made compromises. But one thing I know for sure is that you never made any"

"But isn't it a good thing on my part?" I questioned his observation

"In professional and materialistic issues, yes that is. But in emotional issues it is not. A relationship stands on three pillars. LOVE, TRUST and RESPECT. If you even have either of them for any person , you will definitely make compromise"

"Will I" I challenged him

"You love your parents, you trust your parents and you respect them too. Am I correct?" he questioned me

"yes I surely do"

"So would you or wouldn't you make compromise for them if a situation arises?"

I had got my answer. I was able to see the picture that Shubho was trying to show me. I had been ignorant all these years to not realize what was in front of me. And also adamant enough to not accept it as well.

"But then how to know which one of my ex-girlfriends was correct for me?"

"None of them" he promptly replied

"And why do you think so?"

"Because none of the relation survived"

"But then how can I be sure that my marriage will survive?"

"No one can be sure. And hence you need to put efforts to make it survive."

"What kind of efforts?"

"The same which I talked about, like compromise, maturity, patience, love, trust, respect"

"But how can I be sure that she will also do the same"

"Frankly speaking, she may not. But in that scenario, you have to show her the path. And you will not be able to show that path if you yourself don't believe in it"

"And is there a way that can guarantee my belief"

"This is not a materialistic issue Daksh. There are no guarantees in emotions. The maximum you can do is to find a girl whom you will definitely like for her qualities and for whom you will be willing to lead the path"

"But always it turns out that I do like a girl but never end up loving her"

"One thing I can guarantee Daksh, that none of your girlfriends shared the same qualities. But then try to figure out the top three qualities which you liked in your previous relationships and what you will like to see in your life partner"

"That sounds like a good start point. That I can do"

"But remember" he warned me "also note down the top five qualities which you don't like at all, which you cannot stand at all and which definitely you wouldn't like to see in your life partner"

"That's easy I think"

"If you believe me, and mark my words, no it is not."

"and why do you say so"

"it is because the good things have to be majestically big before you start appreciating it, but the bad things have to be minuscule for you to start getting irritated. And many a times you don't even know what irritated you"

I was already thinking

"I think I have already given a lot of *gyaan* for you to think about. Now it is my term to give some *pyaar* to my dearest wife" he said with a mischievous tone.

"Oh yeah. Sorry I kept you away so long. Convey my sorry to *boudi*"

"Don't worry. She understands that friends need some personal time too"

"Thanks man for hearing me out patiently and clearing my doubts"

"Actually I am doing a favor to myself" he said in a hushed voice. He continued "once you get married, I believe our better halves can bond over complaints about us, while we can go live our younger days"

I couldn't stop myself from laughing aloud. Once I kept the call, I knew I needed some serious thought. But first I required a strong filter coffee and a cigarette puff. I could feel the younger Daksh back in my veins.

Men at work

The next day when I reached office, I had a pile of mails waiting in my inbox. I slowly read each one of them, trying to ignore the non-important ones. I made a list of the important ones on my desk and assigned them a priority number. I love to be systematic in office work. Everything gets a priority number and no task jumps its priority number, until and unless I am stuck with a dependency on someone else for that specific task. As a habit, I then went to the cafeteria for my breakfast. I ordered an egg sandwich and a cup of ginger tea, while still deliberating the response needed to write for Nick's mail, our company's sales representative working in Brazil. I squeezed out tomato sauce by the sandwich and walked down to the extreme corner table overlooking the parking lot and the busy highway. On my way I ran up to Pooja. She waved a big Hi and I could see a big smile on her face. It was apparently awkward, as we hadn't spoken since our breakup a year back. I did respond with a very well calculated smile but continued in my stride. Apparently she followed me and came up to my table, and as soon I took my chair she spoke "I just wanted to say that I am getting married next month. And it was all possible because of you."

"Well congratulations", I responded. I was not very sure what my response should have been, but I was not able to figure out what she meant.

"I think you did not understand", she continued "once we broke up I knew that I deserved much better in life. That was a relationship which gave me the opportunity to think seriously about my life and my expectations out of it. Whatever done I will always be thankful to you", she paused for a moment. I could see a frown taking over her smile. Deep within I knew she was searching for an appropriate synonym for me, but I believe, being in an office environment she controlled herself. And as expected of her she turned around and thumped back towards the cafeteria entrance.

"Well it was my pleasure to show you the correct direction in your life" I shouted sarcastically to her back. She would have preferred to show me the finger but instead she flashed her fists up in the air to show her disgust.

I sat their sipping my tea, thinking about the unexpected start of the day. But soon I was pulled back to the list of tasks waiting at my desk. I quickly finished my breakfast and walked back to my desk.

Like all days I left office at six in the evening. Went home and changed to my jogging tracks. I hate jogging in parks where people come of all ages and speeds and the jogging tracks get crowded. I prefer jogging along the lanes of my colony where I find peace with myself. This is the time of day when I do not think anything. I don't even carry my cellphone or an ipod. When finally after a jog I reached home at eight thirty, my cook, Raghu was preparing my dinner, and my protein shake was kept on the center table. I took a sip of the shake and went for a quick bath. Once I was out I finished my shake and switched on the news channel on TV. Raghu was done preparing my dinner and he also left. I sat there browsing the news and sometimes swapping it back and forth with Discovery channel. Around nine I had my dinner while watching discovery channel. Once done, I picked up an Agatha Christie's novel and read it till I dozed off. Next couple of days went the same, and I did not get time to think anything else outside my schedule.

On Thursday, I got a call from Piyush. He wanted to meet over to discuss on something urgent. Since I was busy with my office work and couldn't talk, I invited him over for dinner. When I came back from my jog in the evening, he was already sitting on the couch in my living room sipping a cup of tea, while Raghu was preparing dinner. I had called Raghu earlier in the evening asking him to make something delicious with potato and a chicken side dish for two people. I had sensed anxiety in Piyush's voice and I knew spicy potato and a chicken side dish are his weakness. It smelled delicious. I quickly took a bath and joined him in the living room. The dinner was ready and Raghu had left for the day.

"You want to eat first or talk?" I enquired

"Can we talk first?" he said

"Sure. Tell me"

"This is about one of my colleagues, Akruti" he continued "she is beautiful, sweet and very funny. We had hit off pretty well and I was even looking ahead into a relationship, but recently she has been trying to avoid me. It is very difficult on me" he spoke in a single breath.

I took a pause and looked straight in to his eyes. I was rather amused. Having known him all my life, he had never reacted this way for any girl. His outlook towards girls could be best described as that of an eve teaser and one who can without any shame ogle at any girl at any place of the world. He has been funny all his life but he never had the maturity to be in a relationship and appreciate it. I myself was taken aback. I did not know how to react to his apathy. I trusted my instincts and went ahead with a very professional way of dealing this by first uncovering the ground reality.

"How long have you both known each other!! And why is that you have never mentioned this girl to any of us"

"She joined as a fresher into my team some three years back. She was not so pretty or hot that I would pass comments on her. But slowly we ganged up as a team and started complimenting each other in all wild adventures and pranks"

"But you always mention every girl you see every day for I don't know how many years, but you never spoke of this girl in spite of knowing her for three years now." I was seriously feeling cheated.

"Yeah I did not. It actually never occurred to me. I never considered her as a girl. She has always been the cool dude buddy of mine in office"

"And when did you start getting feelings for her?" I enquired

"I don't know. I never realized. We have always been a pair in crimes and always hanged out together. Even after office hours we are always in touch on messages and calls and we know each other's whereabouts at all times. But recently she has started acting awkward."

"So it will be frank enough to tell, that you started having feelings only when she started to have her own individual life as well, unlike earlier" I questioned him

He looked broken. He did not want to accept the fact, but he took a deep breath and said, "I guess so"

"Hmmm" I responded. Once I had my ground reality established, I asked him further "And what do you expect from me?"

"I want answers. You have been the champ among us who has always found the better way with girls"

I did not know whether to feel proud of this fact or be ashamed of the fact that even after so many relationships I am still searching for the answers myself. But that was a different war all together with myself, and I preferred to keep it within curtains. To give a response, I preferred to keep my funnier side away and let my mature side answer. After Shubho's talks I did realize I had a mature side which I had kept hiding behind my layers of ignorance. "You cannot categorize girls. Treat them as individuals. Yes they all have some common traits which the Mother Nature has used to define them. But that does not mean they do not have their individual likes and dislikes."

"I will tell everything about her so that you understand her likes and dislikes"

"It is not that simple Piyush. You have been her buddy for last three years and you still claim you do not understand her. How do you expect me to understand her just by a mere description about her!!"

"I don't know all this. I want you to teach me steps to win her" he spoke adamantly

I was aghast by his sheer insensitive attitude. I collected myself and responded, "The first rule is to be true, to be what you are. There are no steps. If it clicks at both ends, the relationship flourishes"

He didn't seem quite satisfied with my answer. He wanted a step to step guide which he could follow to the point. I could understand his situation. He was in a panic with the fear of losing this girl, so I thought of helping him out so that he can find his own way.

"Tell me one thing Piyush. Have you ever proposed her, or told her that you like her or given any hints that you would like to take the relationship into next level", I asked

"Isn't that obvious when a boy spends so much time with a girl?" he responded immediately

"That means you haven't. And as a matter of fact it isn't obvious. This is no engineering question that logic will uncover the mystery. It's about emotions. It takes years to build a relationship but only a moment to lose it"

I could see his expressions change while trying to figure out the meaning of the sentence.

I continued," as you said you have been buddies for so long, has it ever happened that you have passed judgments on some third girl based on her looks, while she was around. Or passed some comments which portrays shades of lust"

He smiled for a moment as if he remembered some funny occasion, but soon the fact dawned on him and with a very shy smile he said, "I guess many a times"

"Don't you see that in spite of all these she stayed around you. Her likes for you were far beyond to neglect these immature acts of yours"

"So you mean to say she loves me", he asked with a very hopeful voice and a smile breaking off his lips

"I didn't say that. It is just a speculation" I clarified

"Then why didn't she tell me"

"Because the girls expect the boys to propose"

"And why so? Why are they so heavy heads. Why can't they say if they like someone" he objected in a childish fashion raising his arms up in the air

"They may, but what I am saying is that most of them won't. They expect the boy to be a man enough to make her feel like a princess, whom he loves and will take care of, one who will pamper her and who will just be hers'."

He wanted to say something, but before he could I added, "This is the way God has made them, and appreciate them with this mindset"

"But what has this to do with the boy proposing?" he asked raising his hands again in animation. Knowing him for so many years I knew he is on the verge of losing patience. He has to be calmed down, and hence I quoted "may be they want to see the nervousness and the fear of losing in the boy's eyes".

Very seriously he tried to analyze the statement before he realized the pun hidden. And we both had a small laugh. I was really hungry now and I started plating the dinner. He stood beside watching me, but I knew he was thinking something. He suddenly crackled up. I looked at him, and he said, I know why girls don't go down on their knees to propose a boy. I asked , "Why"

"Because the boys being boys will start unzipping their pants as soon as she goes down on her knees", and we both laughed aloud. I was happy that he was still in his wits but a bit scared also that in this serious issue also he was thinking of such jokes.

After a few moments of silence, he did ask, "so you want me to go and propose her?"

I tilted my face to my right to have a look at him and shook my head in negative. This action was more than enough to confuse him and he thumped his fist on the table in irritation. "a couple of minutes back you asked me to be man enough to go and propose her and now you are asking me not to"

I spoke again "A propose should not be done for the sake of proposing"

His lips twitched up on the left side, his forehead squeezed and eyes widened, as a classic Indian expression of being confused.

I continued, "You are not East Clintwood, that you will walk over to a girl and propose, and she will feel weak in her knees and give you a tight hug and a kiss"

He could feel the sarcasm and understood the meaning. He asked, "so what should I do?"

"I don't know exactly what you should do. Actually I am not even sure of her sudden change of behavior as you are saying. It could be that she is going through a personal issue", I waved my hands in a gesture to offer him a seat and placed the dinner plate in front of him, "or that she is getting pressure from home to get married. Any girl can feel tense in that situation. It could be that she actually liked you and waited long for you to propose and now has given up to pursue other options" his eyes were happy partly because of the possibility of her liking him and partly because of the chicken leg piece in his hands, "or that you may have pissed her unknowingly on something". He stopped biting the leg piece for a while as if trying to figure out something of his past interactions with her.

After a few seconds he spoke again, "I am clueless" and in a posture with his palms attached and forwarded towards me, *"raah dikhao baba"*(show me the path Senor).

I laughed a bit, trying to figure out something. The rest of the dinner went quietly, he gorging on the potato curry and chicken, and me thinking over a strategic move. After dinner we went over to the terrace. Once I knew I had his attention, I spoke "I will suggest you a few steps. But you may need to improvise. You have to be alert to understand her reactions and agile enough to maneuver the interaction." With his affirmative head movement I knew he was with me. "Tomorrow is Friday. After office hours, try to take her out for a walk. Prefer a non-congested road where you can get more time to talk"

"What kind of talk" he asked

"Talk about anything common or interesting. Be yourself. Be the witty and the crazy one whom she first met. But do not talk about emotions or likes or anything depressing. And nothing about any other girl, even if Angelina Jolie passes by", I know he worships Angelina. I was laughing within.

He said "OK" in a very serious note, completely missing my pun.

"Does she have any liking for a particular food, mainly any street food or fast food" I enquired

"Yeah she loves *paanipuri*"

I could feel the excitement within me "Wow", it is what I had thought about. I continued, "make sure you stop by a good street side *paanipuri* stall. Make her comfortable around you"

I thought a little, and then added, "after that in the night try dropping her home"

On hearing this, he immediately replied, "don't ask me to do the coffee act"

A bit irritated about such low expectations out of me, I continued, "Listen first before reacting. On the way back, suggest going for the new Shahrukh Khan movie on Saturday evening"

"Shahrukh Khan.. Yikes" he replied. He has never been a big fan of Shahrukh Khan or his movies. He prefers Salman Khan and Govinda movies which are usually conned as *masala* flicks.

"Plan a day for her, idiot, not for you. Girls love Shahrukh and his romance. Don't ask me for the reasons. And try for an early evening show"

"And then what.. I sleep in the movie hall, while she enjoys"

"I hope you can show some interest on what she likes. She has shown interest for three years on what you like" I retaliated as if advocating for Akruti. He understood my intentions.

I continued, "try watching the movie through her eyes. Be genuine, and please do not fake to go an extra mile to impress her. If possible try holding her hands in yours."

"that will be too much" he objected

"If you love her and want to spend rest of your life with her, this is nothing. And doing so, will un-officially signal your likings for her. And if during an intense or romantic scene, she holds your hand harder, that is the sign you should look for"

"And what does that mean?" he enquired

"It means she looks you as a support and likes you too"

"OK. Got it", and he stood up with a smile on his face, as if the conversation is over. That he has got his doubt clarified and he can handle things on his own. On multiple previous occasions I had been at the receiving end of his extra smartness, and I knew this could be catastrophic. I asked him to sit, "It's not over hero"

"Oh I thought that's it"

Appalled by his innocence, I sarcastically hit back "So if you know she likes you, you just get back to your old terms. And just in case she doesn't, you just walk off the movie hall?"

"No I didn't mean that", he said in his defense.

I rolled my eyes over but preferred to finish of my plan description. "After movie, try taking her to a good restaurant with a good food and more importantly a good ambience. Don't take her to those cheap romantic restaurants though"

His face expressions again changed to show his inability to understand, but I tried ignoring it and while keeping a soft hand on his shoulders continued, "Book a table in advance, and just for a change, be a man to pay the bill. Carry your card."

He gave a sheepish smile reminding me of all those occasions where we had to pay for his food, a couple of times even on his own treat.

"Make her feel comfortable, and if she enquires about you being a changed man for the day, just try giving any funny answer but the obvious. If the time feels correct and you like to propose, find a flower or anything. May be a spoon or may be a tissue paper, just whatever you could find naturally there, sit on your knees and propose her"

"On my knees!!! In a public place!! It will be so awkward, and I have never done this before" he said defensively.

"If you can, it means you are not faking. You are expected to be nervous doing that. If you are not, then you are just doing it for the sake of projecting it as something romantic, and you don't mean it a bit. And it also means that the lady is by far more important person for you and you do not care of the people or surroundings, but her"

I could still see his face expressions change as if deliberating the situation. Understanding his in-convenience, I said, "otherwise, you may also switch the discussion towards romance and ask for her feelings"

His expression changed on the positive side as this was much acceptable to him. But I preferred to warn him "And if the situation does not call for, do not propose. Keep it for some other day. Unless and until you feel confident about your feelings and her reaction, don't do it half-heartedly."

He sat there for a few minutes trying to figure out all the things we have discussed over last couple of hours. We discussed a few more minutes, before he left for his home. It was half past eleven in the night when I finally came to bed. I was happy that I could be of some help to Piyush, and I wished things go fine for him. But I was still not clear about myself. My bad run with relationships had taken a huge toll on my confidence for marriage. I had been so hopeful for all my relationships, but the end came either very quickly or after some few good days of companionship. I started thinking over the sweet ones, Alia and Torsha. It reminded me of some good times. And slowly I drifted off to my sleep.

The Joker gets Cinderella

Next Sunday morning I woke up to a phone call from Armaan. He was standing outside my house for quite some time now, and it seems I slept through all the doorbells. I woke up and let him in. A new continental restaurant had opened near our home a couple of weeks back, and the previous evening we had made plans to go there for a British breakfast. I quickly got ready and we left for "English Daily". To give it an Indian touch, and to please all the major religion sentiments within the country, beef and pork items were replaced by chicken. We ordered scrambled egg with fried bread and butter, chicken sausage, mushrooms, and roasted tomato. He preferred Indian filter coffee, while I ordered for the classic British Twinings tea. The breakfast was delicious as well as sumptuous.

While having breakfast I told Armaan about Piyush and Akruti. He also could not believe that Piyush could keep such a big secret from us for so long. We even called up Arpit to tell him about this development. We planned to have some fun and hence planned to meet near the lake around five in the evening. During our college days, we used to sit by this lake for hours. This was one place we all came to have our time away from the rush of the city.

Armaan and me reached the lake a few minutes after five. Arpit and Neha were already sitting on the rock facing the lake. Neha had kept her head on his shoulders and he was playing with her hair. I could never figure out that when they both loved each other so much, why they always fought on every petty issue. Armaan gave a honk to let them know of our presence. The moment they came down the rock and started walking towards us, Armaan playfully shouted "get a room, lovebirds". Neha didn't take the comment quite well and her eyes narrowed down on him. Arpit sensing trouble held her arms and replied back, "very soon we will". Neha looked into Arpit's eyes and they both started blushing. That moment Piyush came in his Suzuki dressed in a black jeans and a yellow T-shirt. On the pillion was a girl wearing a black sleeveless turtle neck top, blue jeans and a black sandal. Her hairs were tied in a clean knot behind her head and a pair of goggles over her eyes. We had not expected him to have company. As he stopped his bike, he removed his helmet and shook hands with Armaan and Arpit. In an Indian way of holding palms against each other in front of the chest he greeted Neha with *Namaste Ji* and a smile. I stood a few steps behind observing the lady and the un-ending smile on Piyush's face. I stepped forward and hugged Piyush while saying, "this must be Akruti"

Piyush said, "Folks this is Akruti" and then introduced each one of us to her. Armaan shook her hands and with a smile he said, "Piyush has told so much about you. Finally we meet". The next moment he looked at Piyush with a blank face and rolled over his eyes.

Piyush responded with "All's well that ends well". We all were happy for him. Akruti was really beautiful and had a subtle charm. When she removed her goggles, her eyes had an innocence of a child. It was a bit awkward for her to meet the complete gang at once, but it was quite evident that she was an open and fun loving personality. She would fit well in our gang. A nice addition indeed.

Over the next hour we introduced her with the Piyush we knew and discussed embarrassing stories from his past. She also ganged up with us against him. Piyush was sitting quietly with a big smile and a calm face, watching Akruti smile. He was indeed in love. Quite a few times, she looked back at him with narrowed eyes followed with a blush. She looked even happier than him.

Neha asked "So how did this all happen"

Instead of Piyush, Akruti started to elaborate. Piyush had done each and every bit as I had told him. While she was describing this all, Piyush was looking at me with an admiration. As Arpit and Armaan too were aware of all these details, we all four shared a small moment of smile with our eyes. The only place where Piyush had applied his brains was the prop he had used to propose her. It seems he was so nervous that he was playing with the complimentary salad, and he had proposed her with nothing but an onion ring. As our old friendship custom, Armaan, Arpit and me stood up in attention and gave him a military salute. We all fell off laughing.

Suddenly Armaan said that Shubho was missing. Post his marriage we four only used to gang up and Shubho used to join us very occasionally. Post his marriage we preferred to let him have his personal time. With a unanimous decision I was asked to call up Shubho.

"Hey man.. Whats up"

"Nothing. You tell me" he said

"We all had ganged up near the lake, and we were missing you and Ruchi. So we thought of calling you up"

"You should have told me man, we would have also joined"

"We are giving you a chance" I continued, "If you are at home, we all are coming down. We have a very big surprise"

"What surprise?"

"Something which you would have never thought of"

"Oh is it!! We are waiting. Come quick" he said

"In an hour" before I kept the call.

Shubho resides at the other end of the city. Being a Sunday we actually could reach his house in just over an hour. On our way we stopped at a liquor store and bought couple of bottles of the most expensive wine we could get, to celebrate the occasion. We knew that Shubho must have had some added stock at home. When we reached the building watchman gave us a welcome smile. Earlier we all used to live in the same house before Shubho got married.

Shubho lived in the second floor. We all asked Akruti to hide in the stairs area, while we make up her a grand entry. We all made a queue in an ascending order of height before pressing the call bell. As he opened the door, Neha who was standing in the front gave a military salute before entering the house in a march past fashion. Piyush entered next followed by Arpit, me and Armaan. We had a habit of coming up with these instantaneous craps. But deep within, all of us loved such creativity. As we settled down, Ruchi asked

"So what is the surprise?"

"We will give you two chances to guess" replied Neha

"Is your marriage date finalized", Ruchi asked immediately looking at Arpit and Neha

"Soon it will. But now you are left with just one choice"

"Armaan finally bought his car", Shubho said enthusiastically. Armaan had been saving money to buy an Audi. We know it to be a very distant dream but we always keep him driven for his dream.

Piyush was getting restless to tell the surprise and walk Akruti in, but Armaan held him back by his arms. Finally Arpit said, "We have a new addition to our group". As a first reaction Shubho and Ruchi looked at Neha. Arpit soon realized the situation, and said "No not like that. First let us get married, and then we will do family planning". We all had a laugh. He continued, "Someone is standing outside and we will bring her in. You have to tell what is she doing here and how does she belong to the group"

While Arpit and Neha walked towards the main door, Shubho and Ruchi looked at us, "so one of you have got a girlfriend" they looked at me for a moment and said "it cannot be you"

"Why not me?" I protested

"Because of the talk we had this week and your past, Mr. Lady's man. If it was you it wouldn't have been a surprise" Piyush and Armaan were laughing at me.

Arpit and Neha walked in with Akruti and introduced them to Shubho and Ruchi. Neha kept on with the guess game. Shubho and Ruchi tried to figure out hard. Piyush was getting excited, and to make matters worse for the Bengali couple in the guess game, Armaan started imitating Piyush's excitement.

Finally Ruchi spoke, "the thought of either of you getting such a beautiful girlfriend is in itself a big disbelief. Why don't you only admit and surprise us"

We all laughed a bit, and Akruti looked with a blushed smile towards Piyush. Shubho observed this and moved ahead and gave Piyush a hug.

Ruchi gave Akruti a tight hug instead. For the next half an hour or so, the new pair remained at the pinnacle of focus and all conversations. Shubho and Armaan took a smoke break at the balcony. Over puffs Armaan told Shubho about the story of the new love birds and my involvement as a guide.

When they came back, the wine bottles had opened up along with some beer cans and a vodka bottle and everyone had a glass in their hand. Shubho and Ruchi went inside the kitchen to quickly arrange for some scrambled eggs and snacks. A while later we ordered for pizza. By the time we were done with pizza, the girls had moved into the bedroom leaving the boys by themselves. Shubho was pulling my legs about me calling him up to take advice about marriages and on the other hand giving free guaranteed consultations to others.

Suddenly Akruti came out of the bedroom into the hall and stood in front of me. Even though she had quite a good amount of wine, she was still in her senses, her eyes narrowing down on me.

"I thought it was him who proposed his love to me, but now I find it was all you", her eyes were still narrowed down on me.

Piyush spilled over his wine in disbelief. We all froze for an instant. The sense of guilt hit me really bad. But something inside me was telling that if I don't handle this now, it will be over for ever. I knew Arpit hadn't told Neha about this, so it has to be Ruchi who must have told her. And it had to be Shubho who told Ruchi. For a

flash second I stared at Shubho. Even Armaan had figured out the same and he was staring at Shubho. Shubho's eyes met with mine, then with Armaan's. Ruchi and Neha had also come out of the room. Shubho looked at Ruchi helplessly. Looking at Ruchi it was quite evident that she was a bit high and cannot be blamed for divulging the information. I tried to focus back on handling this situation first.

I took a long breath and very calmly replied, "Would you have expected this idiot to realize it himself" while pointing at Piyush who was trying to wipe out the spilled wine from his cloths.

Her gaze was fixed at me, but her eyes narrowed even further as if she is thinking something. She replied "No. I had actually myself given up on him", and she looked at Piyush with an emotion that could be best described as a mix of anger, sympathy and love. She smiled a bit and then asked again, "How did you know that I will say a yes. Did you stalk me or did some research on me!!"

Sensing she has sobered down a bit, I managed to give out a little smile. "How else can you expect me to belief that a beautiful girl like you is still hanging out with an utterly hopeless idiot like him".

Piyush narrowed his eyes on me, while we all burst out laughing. He walked over to Akruti, kissed her cheek and wrapped his left arm around her back. It was a nice change for us looking at the protective, more self-assured Piyush, but knowing him for so long led us to have another blast of laugh for this action.

She added "so I understand you know him pretty well, and you are the person whom I need to talk to in case I go crazy by his nonsense acts"

I instantaneously replied, "and also whom he needs to walk to if he feels the other way about your sophistication".

Piyush pouted and we all laughed again. Sensing the situation has been handled pretty well and things are back to normal, I could calm down a bit. I gave out a long breathe and gulped the rest of wine present in my glass in a clean single shot down my throat.

Ruchi came down and sat near me. She was quite high. She looked appreciatively in my eyes, and said "It seems you have matured enough to take care of a girl and give her the respect of a wife." I smiled back with pride, before she continued "so when can we meet the *Dakshi* of *Daksh*". Shubho as if was waiting for this moment, jumped over my shoulders and shouted "get me a *boudi*".

Armaan who was closely watching this replied, "You have a wife man, why do you need a boudi?"

In a flash second, Ruchi was slapping Armaan's back, while Shubho was trying to punch his shoulders. Akruti and Piyush stood by the side laughing all along.

While this was going on, we heard Arpit and Neha quarrel over some issue by the balcony. It seems Neha wanted to know that if Arpit knew of my support to Piyush in his endeavor, why she was not taken into confidence by him. She felt bad to know about this from Ruchi. She expected him to tell her everything, just like how Shubho tells everything to Ruchi.

Armaan, Piyush and me looked at Ruchi at the same instant and spoke in unison "No grudges against you *boudi* but", and we pounced on Shubho with friendly punches all over his body. Akruti and Ruchi shared a quiet smile between them, and I could not avoid noticing it. It seemed they spoke telepathically in that moment that they knew how to get secrets out of men, and what Neha is doing is just another approach.

Once satisfied with our efforts on Shubho, we turned to Arpit's rescue. By now Arpit was in pacifying mode, trying to make her believe that he didn't know anything about it, and he was equally shocked to hear the revelation. And that he would never think of hiding any information from the love of his life. Neha on the other hand was telling him that she saw his reaction when Akruti came and told the truth to me. She knew that Arpit was an equal partner in crime. Armaan stepped in and said that I told him everything on the bike while we were coming to Shubho's house. And as Arpit was with Neha in a different bike, so there is no way Arpit would have known this without her being aware of. He also added that he told Shubho about this over smoke in the balcony while Arpit was with her. And that Arpit's reaction on Akruti's revelation can be justified because he knows us for so long that it was not a surprise for him. It seems she bought our story and calmed down a bit. But she was still angry with Arpit.

The girl gang was back with their meeting in the bedroom. We all stood in the balcony. Shubho offered us cigarette. The day had been full of ups and downs, and we desperately needed a puff. Though it was evident that Arpit wanted to have one, but he declined the offer. Armaan commented back to him,

"Hey why are you always so afraid of Neha?"

"It's not about being afraid. It is more about a way to do something what your lady expects out of you. And more importantly what I expect is peace" Arpit spoke in defense and tried to give a smile.

"So why don't you get a girl who loves you for what you are and doesn't want to change you?", Arpit tried to talk sensible

"Because, it is never possible. Girls fall in love with you and your qualities. Then she makes a list of your non-qualities and makes sure she eradicates them from you" he spoke. Shubho and me nodded affirmatively.

Arpit continued, "So what if she is dominating and we fight so much. Tell me one couple who doesn't", Piyush pointed towards Shubho as if trying to bring our attention to Shubho and Ruchi.

Shubho replied with a sad face and a pout, "even we do fight, but we know when to stop and when not to fight, like not in front of friends and family". He gave an ear to ear smile with pride.

Arpit continued, "A relationship is not a fair-weather companionship. For a relationship to work, you need to be around when either one is down and has nothing good to offer but anger or tears or frustration. You just stand there as a support and as a companion for the bad weather to pass off. And the more quietly and peacefully you do it, the relationship gets more cemented"

Armaan took a couple of steps back and looked at all of us "I am so proud that you all have matured so much, but I miss my old duffer friends"

Arpit replied back, "My dear boy, what I told you is not maturity. It's the cunning experience of being in a relationship. You need to talk like matured, because that is the smartest thing to do when you know she is hiding a probable tricky test just around some corner. It's better to keep reminding yourself of the learnings and tricks, rather than always stand at the firing line after failing the test". Shubho and Arpit gave each other a high five.

Then with a hushed voice Arpit said, "Since we are already in this topic, I will give you an added *gyaan* for life. Girls always use three deadly weapons to win a conflict"

"And what are they", asked Armaan impatiently

"First, she will test your endurance and patience! It means she knows that we boys love to get over fights as quickly as possible and move on with life. But on the contrary they like to stretch the fight as long as possible. Actually in ideal world, they never want the fight to end till we accept our defeat. And they will come up with all those topics which you don't even remember ever happened or existed. This is what was happening now some time back between me and Neha, and it would have continued to eternity if you all would have not stepped in. But trust me, it's not over yet. It will resume again when we get home" and he gave a sad smile. We patted his shoulders in support, and gave an assuring smile.

He continued, "Second is the timing of the fight. They will wait for the moment when they are sure you are not prepared or are very tired. The deadly time zones of fight are just before breakfast when you are hungry, just after your coming back from office after a bad day, while making love, or just after you are back from a workout, and the most important, when you are watching your favorite match on TV, or playing your favorite video game."

We all tried to remember our past experiences, and nodded affirmatively.

"And third and the most powerful are tears. When they are pretty sure that you have managed to successfully counter the first two deadly weapons of self-destruction, they start crying. They know that you love her and can't see tear in her eyes. And that you will fulfill all their demands just to avoid the tears."

We all patted with support on each other's back and shared a short hug. Shubho spoke, "Women. We can't live without them and living with them is not easy either". We all laughed again.

Armaan spoke, "but if you know all the weapons, you should also know, how to avoid the weapons"

Shubho spoke, "In a natural world, you cannot avoid the weapons, but there are ways to counter the weapon"

"And what are they" Piyush asked enthusiastically

"Best way to win an argument for men is to stop talking and pretend to be listening. A nod for every word. The other option is to say a sorry, hold her hand and give a kiss on her forehead, reassuring her that you accept your mistake and will never let it happen again" Shubho replied

"*Aillaa*, with my memory I may require to maintain a logbook with the details of all my promises", Piyush said innocently

"No use of that. Either you will not realize that you repeated the same mistake, or else she will find out a so called annexure of that promise that you didn't suffice"

"So isn't there any way out" asked Armaan

"There is one" said Shubho

"And what's that?" asked Armaan and Piyush in unity

"Become like Daksh and walk out of the relationship at the hint of a fight", replied Shubho

We all had a big laugh, while they punched my shoulders and acted as if they are taking my blessings. The discussion went on with other boyish talks and was not over before Neha and Akruti came out suggesting it was late in the night and we should leave, and before I acquired a new name *BABA*"

Arpit and Piyush were in senses and they managed to drive back. Armaan was supposed to drop me home in the night, but since me and Armaan had a lot to drink, we both preferred to walk down to his house which was a couple of kilometers away.

It does get serious

Next morning we woke up to a bad head ache. We had some black coffee, before I left for my house in an auto rickshaw. Armaan preferred to have another hour of sleep before he went to Shubho's apartment to ride his bike to office.

The weekend was great and we all had a nice time. I was feeling very relaxed, and in spite of a bad headache, I was able to do work very efficiently.

On Tuesday, Shubho gave me a call to let me know Ruchi is giving a party with an intention for me to meet prospective brides. She had invited all couples and each and every eligible bride known to them. To top it all she had made sure that I am the only bachelor in the party. She wanted me to get introduced to as many girls as possible and then take a decision. On listening to this, I literally panicked. Even though I consider myself easy and smooth to get introduced to a girl, the thought of making a forced choice out of a given set of options, literally paralyzed me. I requested Shubho to convince Ruchi against this. He assured me he will try and I knew what it meant. Still I prayed for the small probability of it getting true. I could not focus much on the office work, for the remaining day. I felt anxious.

In the evening when I came back from jog, Ruchi gave me a call.

"We are planning this for you my dear. And there is nothing to panic about. All the girls present would be directly or in-directly known to me or Shubho, so just trust us and ride along" she spoke as soon I said Hello over the phone. She did not want me to speak or give any excuse. It was typically her style of convincing anyone, by telling them what she wants and then hanging over before you get a chance to object or argue. She continued, "I am planning for Saturday evening at eight. So be there on time" and she hanged up the call. Even though the call was done, I could visualize her and Shubho give each other a high five and share a devil laugh.

After my dinner, I quietly sat watching a football match. I didn't care who the opponents were and what tournament the game was part of. I was happy watching the men dribble the ball. I wanted to divert my attention into anything other than the thought of a party with me as the male protagonist. Though I was watching the men dribble the ball but my mind was somewhere else. I could picture myself as the idiot joker, and the whole party as a comedy circus. What if I did not like anyone? What if I like more than one? What if I become nervous? What dress

should I wear to the party. The sequence of thoughts was overwhelming. I didn't have answer to many questions. I started thinking about my younger days in an attempt to get the answers. Those were the days when I was in relationships of my choice.

The thought of my first proposal brought an innocent smile on my face. My father had shifted town for work, and he got me admitted to a co-educational school. I was pretty excited as my previous schools were all boys school. I was in sixth grade. Every morning after school prayers we were supposed to walk up to our respective class in a queue. At the end of the prayer hallway, a few school monitors used to stand on either side inspecting for proper school dress, tie, belt, shoes, hairs, nails, etc. I used to see this girl everyday standing at end of the hall monitoring the nails. She used to hold our fingers in her palm and inspect them visually but very efficiently. She was three years senior to me. Her name was Smita. I kind of had a liking for this girl which increased to a level of infatuation. I used to make sure that I stand in the queue that she would inspect. I used to make sure my nails are proper every day, in an attempt to impress her with my diligence. It took me a complete year to give a smile, a nervous one though, and say a Hi. While I was in seventh grade, I came to know that post tenth examinations, students leave school and join junior colleges of their choice. This had caused me a panic attack. A few days before the final examinations, during school lunch hour, I took the courage to walk up to her. She was sitting with her female classmates. I looked straight into her eyes. They were the most beautiful thing I had ever seen. Having Bollywood movies as my only guide in this matter, in a similar way, I had plucked a flower from the nearby bush and while holding them in my hand, told her what she meant to me. Her friends laughed at me and made me look petite in my own eyes. She had smiled and looked at me with caring eyes. She stood up, and walked that extra step to stand directly in front of me. She pulled my cheeks with her thumb and forefinger and ruffled my hairs. She spoke that this is not the age for me to get involved into all this, and I should focus on my studies. She also said that I was very sweet of taking the effort to walk up to her and tell her my feelings. But she felt that a few years later when I would grow up a little more, I will get someone more beautiful. And if I won't I should come back and meet her once whenever and wherever possible. With a mixed emotion of nervousness and excitement, I ran back to my classroom in full speed. The next few days I was lost in my own world of dreams, my face dawning a mixed smile of shyness, achievement and eternity. My eyes were hopeful to meet her sometime soon in the future. It took me a few more years to get over her, till I met Priya in my junior college.

I am still in touch with Smita, and she is a very good friend of mine. She is happily married with two beautiful kids. We talk sometimes on phone, and many a times she makes fun of my innocence, making up for what she missed on that day.

My thoughts wandered more and led me to the thought of Alia. She was the sweetest and the funniest person I ever came across. She had an oval face, blue eyes, thin eyebrows, and thin pink lips. Her long thick black hairs always fell on her back in a neat orderly way. Her voice was like a melody. She spoke highly about arts and the brighter side of life. She used to be always optimistic and calm. She was the best thing that happened to me. But destiny had other plans. Now when I look back, I wish the relationship to have matured, but back then I had screwed up pretty bad.

Shubho had asked me to make the list of what three qualities I will look for in the person to get married. Alia was definitely the one who I would have loved to get married to. But then what was that quality in her for which I liked her. What was the one word to best describe her! Beauty! But my other girlfriends who were much prettier, were best forgotten. Was it her being optimistic! Well that one does qualify for my list, but even if a person is not always optimistic, that was fine with me. Was it her love for life and arts! But why should that be. I myself am inclined towards arts, but my choice is more of the crazy ones. She was a more sophisticated one. Would that be a turn on for me? I was not quite sure. Her sweetness! Yeah that must be it. That brought a smile on my face. It was because of her sweetness, I never felt that she was taking away my freedom or my way of living. She was never dominating. She simply could not be one. Her soft nature was my turn on. I still remember if she didn't like anything she would just pout and look at me. She will softly tell that in my ears, softer than anyone could hear. She never cribbed about anything. She was just happy with it or without it. I quickly noted it down in my phone.

LIKES

1. SOFT and CUTE – no dominating, no cribbing

I felt proud to finally come up with one on the list. I eased down a little on my couch and spread my legs across the center table, and switched off the TV. I wanted to add the other two qualities to the list. Also I had to think of the five qualities for my *dislike* list. But the question that kept popping within me was that why Shubho asked me for only three likes but five dislikes. I didn't have an answer to that.

I tried to make a mental list of my exes in descending order of dislike. Shreyasi was at the top of the list. She was one wild cat. I was attracted to her for her no shit attitude. Soon we had started going out. She never believed in tailoring her sentences and was direct in delivering her words. It didn't matter to her who was at the receiving end. She was blunt to even old people. But somehow I appreciated that. I on the other hand, was always a person who would calculate my words when I had to show my anger. I believed in making sure the message has been delivered about my disliking of certain things, but made sure to not offend the other person. It was opposite attraction at best. One evening when we had gone for a walk in the nearby park, some kids were playing football with a soft mid-size ball. The ball rolled over and touched her leg. It was enough for her to lose her temper. A young kid of around six years of age came running looking for the ball. Very sweetly he looked at us and said a Sorry. For that innocence, even if the ball had hit me on the face, I would have let him go with a smile. But she slapped that kid, and shouted at him. When his friends came to his rescue, she even shouted at them and took the ball away from them. The kids kept on asking innocently for pardon, but she was one crazy girl. The realty dawned at me. How can someone be so harsh on such sweet innocent kids? It also occurred to me that previously she had raised her voice for discontent against me at public places. She had on couple of occasions punched me on my upper arms while having difference of opinions. But I had preferred to overlook those because I was smitten by her. Once I had realized that fact, I was tormented to see her behavior to other people over the next few days. I had decided to break the relation. It was one memorable breakup. We were the center of attraction in a public place as she used foul language and few forgettable gestures to let her emotions out. Usually in a breakup or a failed relationship, the girl gets all the sympathy and the boy gets all "it was expected out of you" looks. But somehow I could self-sympathize without any guilt. Friends never speak ill or evil while one of them is going out with a girl. That's brotherhood. But once the news of breakup was known, all of them came in unity to speak against her. I promised myself of not getting into a relationship with such kind of girl ever in my life again. I even asked my friends to take that extra step away from brotherhood and tell me more often when they feel I am in a *mess*.

I will blame it on destiny, but I could never keep my end of the promise. But my friends did. And I will always be thankful to them.

I opened another note in my phone and penned down

DISLIKES

1. NOT KIND TO KIDS AND NO RESPECT FOR ELDERS

2. TEMPER AND PHYSICAL DISPLAY OF ANGER IN PUBLIC including CRIBBING

3. DOMINATING ENOUGH TO GUIDE MY EVERY STEP AND CUT MY FREEDOM

With one point in the *Likes* section and three in *Dislikes,* I had got the answer to why list of dislikes is bigger than my likes. I realized that for a person like me, living with a person with just one very likable thing is more peaceful and fulfilling than living with someone with hundred likable things but just a couple of irritating habits. And Shubho knew about this fact and hence he gave me such an advice.

I started thinking about the qualities I like in my friends, which makes them special. Well boys have some common special qualities which can be expected only from boys and will nowhere look good in girls. But this thought did resonate a loud truth. I would like to have a friend in my wife. But then I suppose every single soul thinks and expects the same from the spouse. But in spite of the great divide of male-female qualities, I would definitely look for a friendly companion in my wife. A person who knows when and what to speak, one who is always unbiased by the fact that friendship comes first, and one who uses brains over heart in normal day to day life. In short a practical kind of person.

LIKES

1. SOFT and CUTE – no dominating, no cribbing

2. PRACTICAL and FRIENDLY

My thoughts drifted towards my personal life, on a day to day basis, what are the things that irritate me the most. I could count on waiting for someone, dependency on different people, interruption in my *ME* time, food with not a good taste, crazy drivers on road. The list was growing and I realized that how picky I am. But I needed to focus on what qualities I couldn't like in my wife. Being married to someone will definitely put me in a scenario where I have to depend on her, and

that cannot be avoided in a relationship. Though I can discuss this with her, and try to minimize the dependency, I have to live with the fact and avoid my irritation for the same. Regarding food with not great taste, well I can give a hand in cooking or we may go out for something yummy. So we have a solution for that. But what about my *ME* time. It is my time and I love that time. I would not allow anyone to disturb me during the same. But how could I make sure it happens.

This was a puzzle. Definitely if it was not solved, post-marriage that would irritate me, and small arguments may later turn out to be bigger fights. And as a person who loves peace and compatibility over anything else in the world, I would just not tolerate that. After a long thought, I realized that if a person is driven by passion about anything, that person is completely focused on that and the person will also expect no disturbance in that time. And I would like to find a person with such kind of passion in personal life. Someone who is driven by personal ambitions and passions. One who has a life above and beyond the professional work life. But what kind of passion could they be. After much more thoughts, I had my answer. It had to be a person who has an artistic touch, may be like reading books, painting, writing stuffs. Even I like to read a lot during my *ME* time. And Alia was one with such a passion. This concreted my thought, and I penned this down in my phone

---

LIKES

1. SOFT and CUTE – no dominating, no cribbing

2. PRACTICAL and FRIENDLY

3. ARTISTIC BEND – reading books, painting, etc

Satisfied with my efforts to complete this list, I turned my focus to complete the *DISLIKES* list. I tried to use the same approach for this list as well. Rather than focusing on my exes and their qualities that irritated me, I tried to think about people that in general irritate me.

The most irritating people are the ones who could be termed as – *Hypocrites*. These are people who are ashamed of their actual self and hence project themselves as something else. They have a different thinking but just to please the society talk in their words. And this is not about a single person or two. Every other person I meet is a hypocrite, but of different levels. I meet people who by religion are obliged not to eat non-vegetarian food. In actual world they eat and love it, but they won't

accept this in front of others of same religion. I meet people who talk ill about their seniors or colleagues, but the moment they are in a meeting, they behave as best friends. All road side goons and side-kicks who on a daily basis do every evil thing one can possibly think off, but during a religious activity they act as the role-model torch bearers of the path driven by God and the religious texts. I also interact with people who are very negatively biased to some person, his deeds, his way of life, but at the end of the day, these very people are their greatest followers mimicking their every step. These people actually live a virtual life, and as a person I hate them. And I would prefer not to have a hypocrite as my life partner.

The other kinds of people I prefer not to befriend are the ones who do not have their own stand point. They work in a specific way because they have been asked to do so. They speak some very specific stuffs only because that is what they were told to speak. They do not go to a film or a party because they have been asked not to go to places like that. It seems they are the robots whose master sits way back at home and controls every step using a remote. On being asked why they do not take a stand point, most of them claim they do not want to hurt other people who care about them. I have a belief that these are fine till a certain age, but once you are on your own, one should start taking their own decisions. If you don't you are just scared of standing up for yourself. And if one cannot stand for oneself, I belief that person will never stand for anything in life. We are never born with correct decision making abilities. We make some bad decisions that teach us and make us realize our abilities more. Hence I believe we should always keep trying to find our own self. That is how we learn.

I thought about much other stuff too. By the end I realized that as a person I have a very selective fondness of people. I did start getting a feeling that I should meet a psychiatrist to resolve my issues about various kinds of people and their habits. This also gave me a window to peep into the failure of my previous relationships. Sub consciously I had a very definite taste, and I didn't like anyone who didn't fit the order. I took a mental note to be more patient and understanding, but then having sincere eccentric tastes is not a crime. So I re-opened the note application in my phone and penned down

---

DISLIKES

1. NOT KIND TO KIDS AND NO RESPECT FOR ELDERS

2. TEMPER AND PHYSICAL DISPLAY OF ANGER IN PUBLIC including CRIBBING

3. DOMINATING ENOUGH TO GUIDE MY EVERY STEP AND CUT MY FREEDOM

4. HYPOCRITE

5. SPINELESS ROBOTS

By the time I was done with these, I realized it was already half past four in the morning. But I was satisfied that a big task was offloaded from my head, and I felt calm. This task was a necessary foundation for my step towards life's commitment. I needed some sleep now, so I just closed my eyes and eased off into the couch. When I woke up it was nine in the morning and sun was brightly shining into my room. I quickly took a bath and raced to office for an important meeting scheduled for ten o'clock.

Saturday morning I got a call from Shubho reminding me of the party. Once the list was created and me being aware of what all to look out for, I had been upbeat the whole week, and had been looking forward to this party. In the evening I dressed up to look at my best. I wore my favorite khakis with a white linen shirt and a corduroy jacket. I preferred to wear a nice casual loafer. I wanted a classy but a very casual look of myself. I wanted to look something between the professional and the completely outdoor casual sporty look. Once satisfied with my appearance I left for Shubho and Ruchi's house.

When I reached there, I was amazed to see the crowd. The party was in the terrace. I was already a bit late. The details of the décor and the food were well taken care off. Ruchi's pain staking efforts were quite evident. People had come in all kinds of dressings, but men seemed to show an affinity for a casual wear, whilst the women were draped in traditional saris. The Bengali community was in prominence. Though being a part of Bengali community myself, I had no way limited my search to them. Ruchi knew this fact and the variety of cultures was quite visible in the party. For a couple of minutes I stood by the staircase watching the crowd before Shubho noticed me. He came with an extra glass of wine. While offering me the same he said "So are you ready?" I just looked with blank eyes and a sarcastic smile at him. He continued, "You lucky bastard, I never got this chance in my life"

I smiled back at him and said, "It's actually scary and its good that you didn't have to go through this"

He tried to ignore my comment and pulled me into the party. He added though, "If you find someone compatible for me, do get me introduced". I turned to look at him. He winked back at me. My eyes were fixed on him. He added, "For the sake of

old time brotherhood", and we raised our glass to the good old days.

Arpit came rushing towards us. I turned towards Shubho, "You said I will be the only male bachelor, aka , alpha male in this party. What is this knuckle-head doing here?"

Shubho promptly replied, "well even though he is still officially un-married, he cannot be considered one. You would not be sharing territory today"

We both started laughing. Arpit for a moment looked angrily at us but then a shy smile gave way across his face.

We made the corner by the *chaat* counter as our makeshift watch tower. It was a strategic position, as it was far way from the liquor counter and hence devoid of obstruction to our intent. And also for the very well-known fact about affinity of Indian women for *chaats*, we will get a healthy view of the prospects. As in our old college days, we started tagging the ladies with a hypothetical number defining their attractiveness. Any lady below seven was not to be discussed further. Women with *sindur* or *mangalsutra* and Bengali women with *shankha pola* were not to be considered, but just for the sake of Shubho we assigned them a number too. We discussed many of them at a length, and further gave numbers on hypothetical categories like picture perfect quotient, sexiness, oomph factor, fun factor, sensuality, intellect. We further categorized them in girlfriend material, marriage material. We were having fun.

Ruchi came furiously to us and exploded, "What do you think you are doing? Every girl in the party is talking about you three ogling from this corner. Shubho I expected you atleast not be a part of this" She stared at me and said, "and you expect by doing these sorts of nonsense stuff, you will be able to impress one? They don't know why they are here but at least you all know. So please behave."

Arpit was looking down in shame, and Shubho was trying to make his defense. I spoke casually, "Lions first do an assessment for their meal". I wanted to smile at my ill-timed joke, but my eyes went towards the group of ladies from where Ruchi came barging in. They were all staring down at us. In an instinct I turned towards Arpit and said, "how shameful Arpit. You are engaged after all. When will you grow up?". I added an excessive animated display of actions trying to convey the same message across to the ladies. Anticipating this from me, Shubho had also joined in with his animated actions blaming Arpit. And quickly we all dispersed away from there and into the male crowd.

I walked down near the overhead water tank, and lit my cigarette. A kind of heavy guy, dressed in a black suit was smoking a cigar. He turned towards me, and his eyes lit up with surprise and recognition He rushed towards me and gave me a hug, "Hey Daksh, how are you?"

I was still trying to recognize his face through his French beard and the prominent black frame glasses. I was clueless. He pitched in again enthusiastically, "Its me Vikram Arora.. Vicky"

It took me a few moments to actually recognize him even after he gave his introduction. He used to be the Ladies Man back in college days, with his Greek look, long hairs and a well-toned chiseled body. We used to envy him in our first year. Because of him, every other boy was non-existent for the girls in the college. Every girl had just one choice, Vicky. For a small time in second year he was even my role model and I closely watched his every move. I impersonated his moves successfully in the later years to impress girls, and all worked. But that was back then. In the party he was unrecognizable. He was having a double chin, a pot belly, and short hairs with a bald patch at the top. He had changed completely over years. He was looking ten years older than his age. The French beard and the dark glasses were an honest attempt to hide his aging looks. And my thoughts came out loud, "What happened to you?"

"Well in college, I had a life, but I ran out of my quota", he replied followed by a full hearty laugh.

"So what are you doing nowadays?" I enquired

"Well had to get married while I could", he winked and continued "have taken over the family business and nowadays trying to expand it here in Bengaluru"

I was still trying to believe the visible change in him. Not only looks, but his vibrant personality had been taken over by a more matured and materialistic self.

He pitched in, "So what are you up to"

"Well working as a financial executive in a MNC"

"You still look the same man. Married yet?"

"Still lucky I guess", I said and we both raised our glasses.

Shubho came towards us, "So here you are. I have been searching you everywhere" and he gave a formal smile to Vicky. It was quiet evident that he also could not recognize him.

"Shubho this is Vicky" I tried to introduce two old friends again.

Shubho's eyes narrowed on him, and he also tried hard to recognize him, "Vicky from college? No way! I don't believe you?"

Me and Vicky laughed, and keeping hands on his shoulder as an assurance told him, "Just in a new marketing package"

Then a thought dawned on me and I looked at Shubho, "How come the host does not know who all are in the guest list. It is quite evident that you were not expecting Vicky in your party"

Shubho didn't have an answer. Vicky pitched in, "even I didn't know its Shubho's party. It seems my wife and Ruchi are childhood friends, and they ran onto each other a few days back. Hence I was invited with my wife"

Shubho and me said in unity, "Small world indeed"

We started talking about our old college days and the life thereafter. A few steps behind Vicky, there was a very beautiful and cute girl in a blue saree. My eyes kept going back at her. She was talking to a couple of elder ladies.

Suddenly Vicky tapped my shoulders and pointed his fingers to the right, "Isn't that Arpit?"

We turned or heads to that direction, and indeed it was Arpit with Neha. Both were quarreling over something and Arpit's arms were held up near his chest in his typical defensive posture.

"Oh yeah that's Arpit with his fiancé Neha" I said.

"Well it seems his fiance is yelling at him, and he is still the poor kid at the receiving end" Vicky said

"Yeah they have a different love story. The more they love each other, the more they fight" Shubho said

"On his defense though, and on every man's defense, the logic remains the same worldwide" Vicky said. Me and Shubho tried to understand the meaning of his physiological snippet. Sensing our inability to comprehend his sentence, he continued "If a boy yells at girl he is abusive, but if a girl yells at a boy, it's because men are born stupid". We smiled at each other over the obvious gender bias.

A little while later, Ankit came and joined us. He was having a glass of neat scotch. We introduced him to Vicky and even he was surprised. It seems Neha had seen us standing at the corner earlier the night, but she had thought that Ankit and Shubho were just giving me a company. Sure she was correct at first place, but when we had put the blame on Ankit to avoid Ruchi's wrath, Neha had seen our animated

gesture. She was convinced that Arpit was the one ogling at girls and that he wanted to break up the engagement. We all were aware of Neha's eccentricity, but this was too much. If she cannot trust her fiancé and if she cannot differentiate a joke among good friends, it needed a serious look at the relationship.

While we were still deliberating the events and Neha's reactions, Vicky stepped forward towards Arpit, and kept his left hand on his right shoulder and in a very soft voice, said, "Being in a relationship does not mean it has to culminate in a marriage. Sometimes a serious thought is required before it is too late and it has complicated a lot. Say NO when you have to"

Ankit stepped back and with horror in his eyes said, "I love her, and that is why I am marrying her"

Vicky said, "But does she?"

Ankit impulsively replied, "Obviously she does" and looking at Vicky he continued, "And how will you know about these emotions, you never loved any girl, you just used them"

Vicky took a moment to compose himself, then in a very calm voice he replied, "My looks may have changed, but still a part of me likes to win girls. Even though I am married, I do get attracted to other ladies. But I do not try pursuing my thoughts. Do you know why? It is because a few years back I was diagnosed with cancer. Everyone left me but my family and this girl whom I had dumped after just a couple of months of relationship. She stood by me during my treatment. I did win over cancer, but my body took a toll. I was no longer the stud with the look. I was a normal man with average looks. But she didn't leave me. She loved me, and knowing her as a person, even I fell in love with her. We both got married a couple of years back. Still if you look at us, she looks like my daughter even though we have just one year difference in our age. And believe me, I know and understand emotions much more than you do. I have seen the world and people more than you have"

Arpit gathered himself back and said,"what if we fight, it doesn't mean we don't love each other. Yes she has expectations out of me, and I should work to live up to them. When I am not able to, it is expected of her to be angry at me"

"Don't you think for a relationship to grow, both have to understand and be patient? Expectations should be there but more valid ones. If you cannot convince her that you are trying, and if she cannot trust you for these, then I feel something is missing on the compatibility aspect"

Arpit snapped, "You know nothing about her or our relationship. So I won't expect an advice from you"

"It seems this is the first and last girl in your life. Well I have been with so many girls and in so many relationships, just a look tells me a lot. Even Daksh himself will be good in the same. He can second me on that"

I was busy watching the girl in blue saree. I was closely analyzing her every move. She was soft, caring and always smiling. I was drawn to her beauty. I was not even listening to this chat, but when Vicky took my name, I had to get involved in it.

Arpit replied, "Daksh accepts and appreciates my relationship with Neha. And if he had anything to say, he will say to me directly"

Caught completely off-guard, I said, "Neha is a good girl and makes Arpit happy. And I am happy to see my friend happy". I literally blabbered these words just in time to rescue myself.

Vicky held Arpit by his forearms and hugged him, "If you are happy, we are happy". It brought a smile on Arpit's face, but we knew the hug from Vicky was more of sympathy than confidence.

We tried to lighten up the mood and discussed various other topics like, sports, politics, and more importantly about ladies in our lives. Shubho and Vicky made most of the funny comments about marriage, ladies and the married man. This all went for a while, before Ruchi came "Have you just been drinking or would you like to have dinner as well". She then pulled Shubho to the side and in an angry hushed voice said, "Don't forget you are the host and it is your responsibility also to take care of all other guests".

We tried to pretend that we didn't hear any of those words, but Shubho knew otherwise. He smiled at us, and wrapping his arms around Ruchi, he said, "I was just telling these idiots about you and how much I love you"

"Don't lie" she said

"A drunk man can never lie. He always tells the truth" Shubho said while raising his arm with an empty wine glass up in the air.

Ruchi gave us a smile back, and walked away reminding us to have dinner.

We all gave a toast in the air, while Vicky said, "Practice does makes man a perfect liar"

We all laughed and walked towards the dinner area.

Ruchi hushed me to a corner, where no one could hear us. From the corner, we could see the complete gathering. Everyone was busy gorging on the delicious food. Before she could say anything, I complemented her for her efforts, "*Boudi* thanks for taking so much effort just for me."

She blushed, then looking down she spoke, "Actually my party was due for long now. I just gave that party your theme", and then pulled my ears and spoke, "and you preferred to stick only to your idiot friends. You didn't even speak to a single girl"

"Well I was measuring them up" I protested with a smile

"Well two of them enquired about you"

"Is it? Who are they?"

She searched the crowed for a moment and then she said, "ten o'clock, the girl in red top and blue jeans". She further searched for the next girl, and showed, "at the extreme end of your three o'clock in the blue saree". This was the same girl I had been eyeing the whole time.

Very enthusiastically I asked, "This blue saree girl did enquire about me"

"Yeah she wanted to know your identity"

"What you said?"

"Only the good things about you" she smiled.

"What's her name?"

"Aha!! So someone is interested"

"*Boudi* tell me about her" I pouted

"Hmmm!!!" She stared down at me, "Her name is Avantika. She is a software engineer. She is the sister of my college friend Sanhita"

I smiled. While I was still absorbing the name into me, Ruchi held my hands and started walking towards her. She stopped a couple of steps away from where she was having a conversation with a few other young ladies. She called her up by her name in a slightly louder voice. She turned to look at us, and Ruchi, with a hand signal asked her to walk to us.

"Well here is that man in corduroy jacket in person. He is Daksh", said Ruchi

She looked down towards my feet, and gave a shy smile, then as if recollecting her back, she replied, "Well nice to meet you Daksh. But may I ask you Ruchi Di, why are you introducing me to him?"

"It seems this man is as smitten as you", she smiled and patted on our shoulders and walked away. We both gave each other a kind of awkward smile, and tried to look at something else. By the corner of my eyes I could still sense Ruchi, standing at a distance staring down at us calculating our moves. I was bit taken aback by the introduction. I had not expected it to be this upfront and direct. But fact remained that I was really smitten. And I myself wanted to come and introduce myself to her. I took a long breath, and said,

"Well that is what can be expected from *boudi*" I tried to lighten up a bit

She looked blankly at me, as if nothing had happened. I continued "Well I would have taken a different approach"

An interest twinkled in her eyes, and she said, "And what would that be"

"If I would have been Ruchi, and if I walked down to this guy, myself excited about the fact that an extremely beautiful girl draped in blue saree is interested in not so bad looking me, I would have expected me to walk down to you and say – You are not alone"

A smile appeared on her lips, before a calculated blank look taking over, "Alone in what?"

"In being smitten. You look lovely"

"Thank you" she replied with a smile. She continued, "and how would have you expected the girl in blue saree react?"

"Frankly, I would have expected her to shy a bit, her teeth biting her smiling lips and she looking down somewhere at the floor thinking.."

"Thinking about?"

"A quieter and discreet place to talk over a walk"

She looked straight at me for a few moments, and with a mysterious smile replied "Yeah I assume she would have thought exactly the same, but I bet she would had preferred of him to try harder"

"Even though when he knows the girl is interested in him?"

"You cannot believe someone else's word on choice and interest. I believe that's private between two individuals"

"And hence the desire for talk walks, to know more about the individual"

Right then her elder sister walked up to us, spoke something into her ears and left. She thought a little, and then said, "but what if the talk did start but one individual had to leave"

"If the other individual doesn't mind sharing her number, the talk can be continued at a time more feasible"

"Aah, so that will also satisfy the need to the discreteness of the talk, I suppose"

"Exactly" I said with a big grin

We shared each other's cell phone number, before she rushed back to her sister and brother-in-law, who were already near the lift waving a goodbye to Ruchi and Shubho.

Ruchi walked up to me, smiled and said "So how did it go?"

"Nice start I suppose"

"So my party was successful in meeting the desired intentions"

"Well whatever makes you proud" and my fingers were crossed.

Over the next hour everyone left. I too got a taxi back home. I was thinking about Avantika throughout my ride back. She was kind and friendly to people, gorgeous enough for me to literally ogle at, and funny enough to be called again. By the time I reached home, I was very sleepy. I pulled out my cell phone from my trousers' front pocket and wrote a message

"*The person I was talking about wants to talk straight away, but liquor has taken away the best of him. Let him sober up a bit, before I ask the gentleman to call you back*" and I sent it to the newly acquired number of Avantika.

While I changed up to my night clothes, she replied back, "*It would have been better to talk to the actual him while he is in control of spirits, but alas later his polished gentleman identity will be doing the talking*"

I smiled a bit and wanted to reply back, but thought otherwise. A reply to her could wait, but the sleep was rushing in. It had to be attended immediately.

I flow with the wind

Over the next few days Avantika and I shared lot of messages. Her replies were witty as well as funny. A couple of times we spoke on phone as well in the evenings. We had a wide array of common likes and expectations out of life. Slowly we were coming closer. I was really getting interested in her. Every day I was learning something more exciting about her. I asked her out for a date, and as it turned out she was quite excited with the idea. The next weekend we met over dinner. I preferred to keep it formal and slow. This lady was the most sensible and interesting I had come across in a long time. And I didn't want to screw this up. I kept my cheesy pick-up lines at bay, and instead a more matured me had taken over. She had told me that her favorite cuisine was Chinese, and she had tried every good Chinese restaurant in the town. She was looking for something new to please her palate. I suggested for a Thai dinner and she was ready to give it a try. I liked her easy approach and sporty nature.

We met at my favorite Thai restaurant, *Pinto Thai.* While she ordered *khao phat kung*, I preferred *phat thai*. While eating we discussed about international cuisines, travel destinations, Bollywood movies, work life and what not. After main course, when I suggested for dessert, I was happy to see that she was excited for it rather than being calorie conscious. I love to close a meal with a nice yummy dessert, and I like people who love the same. My Bengali genes are to be blamed for that. She browsed the menu and settled for *khanom mo kaeng*. I blindly went for my all-time favorite *sangkhaya fak thong*. She liked her dessert. She even scooped a spoon off my plate as well. In normal get-togethers I would have hated anyone scooping my food from my plate, but surprisingly I liked when she did. I was impressed with her carefree trusting attitude. We enjoyed every moment of our company, and not to mention that the food was as delicious as ever. She also found Thai a good replacement for Chinese cuisine.

After dinner I offered her to drop home. She kept insisting that she would take a taxi home. But I kept pestering till she accepted the offer. My whole intention was to spend as much time as possible with her. In my younger days in college, I had a theory. By the touch of a girl on bike pillion, when she held me for support, I used to determine the feelings of the girl for me. It may sound stupid now, but something within me was waking up the younger Daksh. The younger Daksh was a rash driver as well, but now with the calmness crept in, the ride was smooth. She

sat maintaining a good distance behind me. She had held the bar over the tail light for her support. The road was smooth and the traffic thin. All of a sudden a car swayed into my lane while I was talking over my shoulder with her. I applied brakes in panic, and the bike skidded down to the dusty patch by the road. Luckily the bike was still standing on its two tires and my feet firmly on the ground. Before I could turn and ask if she was OK, she spoke in a soft caring tone into my right ear, "You OK?". I realized she had her hands on either side of my waist, holding me with calm full palms.

I replied, "Yeah I am. You?"

She calmly stepped down the bike, and so did I. I pulled out the side stand, and looked at her. Before I could say something, she said, "These crazy drivers on road are everywhere. You did good to handle the situation."

I was surprised to finally meet a girl who was calm and caring, who did not panic after such an incident. I developed more appreciation for her. I was getting head over heels for this lady. There was a peaceful aura around her and I was getting pulled in. I composed my thoughts, and replied "I should have avoided that"

"Well those things happen. Let's get going"

And so we did. I was still amazed by her calmness in the panic situation. I was trying to focus on road, but my emotions for her were taking over my thoughts. As we were crossing the mall in front of her house she tapped my shoulders to have my attention. She asked me to park my bike in the mall basement. I was surprised by her request, and tried to reason. She just cutely smiled at me. People say boys act crazy, but we can't help when such a beautiful smile shines at us. I didn't ask any further question and parked my bike. I removed my helmet and locked it with the bike handle. I looked at her, she was smiling at me. I asked "What?"

She said nothing. After a moment she slowly walked towards me, and held my left palm with her right, the fingers crisscrossing each other. Her hands were soft and warm. Her left hand held my left arm and she hugged slightly by my side. She stood there for a couple of seconds, as if taking in the feeling. My right hand came over to lift her chin, and I looked straight into her eyes. She smiled and looked down. She spoke, "Shall we walk?"

I smiled. From the day we met I had longed to hold her, but was not sure about how she would react to it. And here we were today walking holding our hands. I was in seventh heaven. I firmed my grip of her hands in mine and we walked towards the mall exit. Over the next hour and half we walked down the colony roads hands in hand. We shared our personal life details with each other. We were smiling all along. She would many a times blush and look down. I was very happy, but deep inside I was scared. She was perfect, but we were getting close too quick. In a week's time from our meeting, we were walking down the colony roads in a dark night, hands in hands. She had so much trust in me, and I was scared of this fact. We were attracted to each other like magnets. I knew a time will come eventually when the attraction will subside and the crude realty of world will creep in. I was scared for that moment. My mind was asking me to enjoy the present but my soul was worried for the future. I think I was in love with this girl but the question within me was asking whether I would live up to her hopes. My history with relationships was no confidence booster.

While I was still thinking all these, suddenly she stopped. I moved another step ahead before realizing that she has stopped. I looked back. Her eyes were narrow but very softly looking at me. She said, "What?"

I shrugged my shoulder, as I didn't know what she was talking about. She slowly lifted my hands a bit which were holding her hands. I realized my grip had firmed while I was thinking. In a very calm voice she spoke, "Don't worry. Things will fall in place. Thinking so much will be of no help." She had read my mind perfectly. I wanted to hug her hard. She was just awesome. I lifted our hands, brought it near my lips and kissed the back of her hand. She literally froze for a moment while a shiver went down her body. She closed her eyes. A few seconds later when she opened them, her eyes were calm and without any reaction. She slowly pulled back her hands, and started walking. I couldn't stop that kiss from coming, but now was feeling guilty and bad for her reaction. Had I taken the step a bit too soon? Should I have waited for the correct moment? My mind was shouting loudly within me, calling me an idiot. But my inner self was congratulating me for doing what was expected in that moment. It knew that even she was scared, as our emotions were flowing freely. But I was getting confused on what I should listen to. We walked in silence while I was fighting between my mind and inner voice. We were standing outside her house, still silent. She was looking into her hands while I was lost with my vision focused a couple of inches above her forehead. I gathered myself, picked her hands while holding her fingers between my fingers and thumb. We stood facing each other, while I spoke "I kept you awake for long, but the Thai food needed time to get digested. Now I hope you will get a good sleep and I can be assured of walking down quietly in your dreams while you sleep tight"

She smiled, still looking down. Her lips parted to say something, but then again kept quiet. She took a deep breath, and then said "I should now get going. Hope you drive back safely"

I didn't want to leave her hands but reluctantly I did let them go. I waved her a goodbye, so did she. She took the stairs for her first floor apartment while I walked back towards the mall where I had parked my bike. A few steps later, I turned around. I wanted one more glimpse of her. Instead I saw a shadow by a window on first floor. The moment I looked up, the shadow was gone. I wanted to believe it was her, but was not quite sure. Deep inside I knew it was her. I turned back and walked away.

Every now and then I took out my cellphone with an intent to message her something soft and romantic, but every time I stopped myself. I did not want to portray my urge and eagerness. When I reached home, I saw a message in my inbox. It was from her,

"Hope you reached home"

"Yeah I did. So what are you doing?" I replied instantly

I freshened up a bit and changed to my boxers and a t-shirt. There was no reply. Her reactions had changed after my kiss on her hands. Her funny and chirpy personality was taken over by a quiet and shy personality. I was still not quite sure whether to consider that a good sign or bad. I sat down on my couch and switched on the TV. A James Bond movie was coming and

Pierce Brosnan was all over it. I didn't realize when sleep took over and I dozed off in my couch.

Next morning I woke up to a loud advertisement on the TV. I realized that the TV had played all night. I picked up the remote and switched it off. There was a sudden silence. I could hear my head pounding. I sat upright. I had a bad backache probably because of the odd position I had slept. I tried to stand up and stretch my body. I walked to the bathroom and undressed myself. I stood still under the shower letting the hot water drip through my heavy head. I turned around and adjusted the shower to pour on my back. I felt good while the warmth transferred from water to my bones and ligaments within me. I was at much ease now. I poured shampoo in my palms and applied them in my head. The coolness of the shampoo and the warm water gave a very soothing effect for my thumping head. I was relaxed and the previous night dawned on me. Every bit of the fun we had and the holding hands and the kiss, and the post Goodnight message. I quickly dried myself and rushed out to reach my cellphone. There was a message from her

"I slept off. Hope you had a nice sleep"

I was rather taken aback reading this message. I had expected more emotions or

excitement. This message was rather plain and short. I didn't know how to react. Was it because of the kiss? It has to be, because she moved inside a shell post that. Her funny self was overshadowed by this expressionless face. But a soft kiss on palms was not such a big deal. It was not like the passionate kiss on lips that may sound as lusty on the first date. This was in fact a kiss of emotion and true feelings. I was just not clear what was going inside her head. The best answer I could convince myself with, was that she was analyzing something in her mind and she didn't prefer to let her words give out any of those thoughts across to me. But I seriously hoped that she gets her thoughts channelized quickly. I wanted to shout out loud that the road on the other side is still rosy. I preferred not to reply immediately. Instead I walked over to kitchen and prepared myself a breakfast of Spanish omelet and bread toast with a cup of coffee.

To keep me distracted, after breakfast I switched on my Xbox and engrossed myself in "Need for Speed" and took out all my anger of the actual road traffic, in the game. I played multiple games till my phone rang. I almost jumped off to grab it, expecting it to be Avantika. Instead it was my mother.

"Did you eat anything from morning?"

"Yes *maa* I had breakfast sometime back"

"Good. So what did you have?"

"Omlete and bread toast"

"That's good. You have learnt a bit of cooking. But wouldn't you like *parathas* or *luchi* for breakfast?"

As appealing as it sounded, I knew where my mother was going with it. I preferred not to respond anything to this. She continued "Write down this number?" she gave me the number and I wrote it down in the notepad by the TV

"Whose number is it?"

"You remember Disha."

"Mamaji's neighbor?" I enquired

"Yeah exactly"

"Why did you then share her number with me?"

"Because I want you to call her so that you both get to know each other better before your marriage"

"I am not marrying her *maa,* I have told you this earlier as well"

"How can you reject a girl without even looking or talking to her"

"So you mean to say that if we go ahead and interact and later find that we are in-compatible, you wont push me to get married to her?"

"What I am saying is that you will love her"

And I gave out a sound out of irritation across the phone. This cannot be ignored by silence or by logic. My mother is convinced and her brother's reputation is at stake. I had no other option but to go ahead and talk to her. I tried to remember her from childhood. She was annoying and moody. I knew I will never like her but I have to give an honest try. "I will call her *maa,* but not immediately. I will do it over one of the coming weekends"

"Why not today?" she enquired

"Because it will sound desperate *maa*" I said in defense. She thought for a while and she accepted my logic. We kept the call after a while after she was convinced that my health was fine, the food I was eating was healthy and that I was taking proper sleep.

I was hungry and my palate was craving for something refreshingly delicious. The first name which came out was Mexican. I had not tried out Mexican food for long, and God I had missed it badly. I quickly got ready, started my bike and off I went to *Mexicana*. I stepped in, and I knew what I was craving for. Without even looking at the menu, I ordered for a Chicken burrito, a tomato chicken quesadillas and a chilled coke. When finally I came out of the restaurant, I was stuffed pretty heavily but I was happy to the core. The food was awesome and fresh.

I called up Armaan. He was at Piyush's house. They were busy playing PlayStation. So I also drove up to his house to intensify the competition. We played a few more games, before the doorbell rang and Akruti walked in. She was very angry to see that we all boys were busy on a PlayStation. Initially I thought that she was angry as did not approve of Piyush wasting time on a game rather than being with her. But it took me some time before I could understand the root of the reaction. The actual reason of her anger was that she expected Piyush to tell her about the PlayStation competition so that she can also be a part of the gang and challenge Piyush. These two souls were perfect for each other and they complemented each other well. They were too engrossed in a sword fight game on the PlayStation. I was happy for them. Suddenly I realized that I had not replied to Avantika's message. So I took out my cellphone and started typing. It took me more than ten minutes to continuously edit my message to her. I was not sure on what stand I should take. It was quite evident that she was interested in me by the way she held my hands. But her quiet self and lack of reaction had kept me hanging in the confused zone. My mind kept on saying I should take things slow, but my heart was excited. As this was a matter of emotions, at the end I let the heart take over the control, and I messaged

"I can still feel your soft hands in mine. It was quite an evening we had. I have a place in mind where the evening requires your presence"

I sent the message and refocused on the match. Akruti was leading by a big margin and Piyush was badly wounded. Another couple of minutes and Piyush had lost by a big margin. Keeping down his wireless controller, he pretended to be sad and spoke to Akruti, "How could you?"

Akruti looked at him, placed down her controller, and looked up again at him. She had a shine in her eyes and her lips twitched to the side. She said, "well haven't you heard what girls do to boys?" and she smiled

"I know about better things though" he said with a pout

"like" and her lips were on his. They kissed for quite some time. Piyush was still not done. He said, "I am still bleeding"

"Aw… my bad", and she planted a series of small soft kisses all over his face, his neck and his hands.

Armaan was quietly watching all this. He looked away and at me. I was smiling at him. I knew he never had a girlfriend and he could never understand these relationship talks. He found them rather unnecessary and idiotic. My smile, actually pissed him off a bit more and he spoke in a loud voice, "Get a room"

Piyush and Akruti didn't hear him at once, but slowly the words dawned at them, and they civilized a bit. They sat down at their chairs with a shy smile. Suddenly there was a complete silence. We all sat quietly. Piyush and Akruti sat there looking at each other, love dripping off their eyes. Armaan sat there lost in his own world trying to act normal. And I sat there thinking about Avantika.

The beep in my phone broke the silence in the room. It was a message from her.

"Are you asking me out?".

I smiled, and replied, "Did it sound otherwise?"

I looked up, and they all were looking at me. Puzzled!! I had not told them about her. And by their reactions it was quite evident that neither had Shubho or Arpit. Armaan finally spoke, "That's a blush we can see on your face. It seems you are back in game"

I didn't say anything. I just smiled back.

Piyush passed a comment "*Bandar kitna bhi budha ho jaaye gulati marna nahi chodhta*"(It doesn't matter how old a monkey gets, he keeps jumping around)

I preferred to ignore the comment while Piyush and Akruti gave each other a high five.

With me in non-committed bachelor territory for a while, Armaan was happy. He had some company for his no-girlfriend club. But this news had hurt him "You had given up on girls. How could you get back?" Armaan protested as if I had broken some law.

"Yeah I had. But then it seems marriage in inevitable. And lately I have been thinking about it a lot. Met this girl and she seemed worth a try"

They all looked at me eager to know more, so I continued "Her name is Avantika. Met her at a party at Shubho's house"

"Wait wait wait!!!.. Party at Shubho's house? When was this? Why weren't we invited?" Armaan spoke anxieted

"Ruchi *boudi* had called in the party last weekend for hooking me up with someone. And it seems she was quite successful"

"Don't expect us to be happy for you when we were sidelined" Said Piyush trying hard to fake his sadness

"Well I hope you are happy with Akruti" and turning towards Armaan, I continued, "this guy is still not ready for girls". Akruti was staring down at Piyush. He was aware of the fact, but he said while wrapping his hands across her shoulders "This here is a fixed account. But Still I can try for current accounts"

I wanted to reply to that, but Akruti spoke before me, "I give you a free hand. I am pretty sure you will not be able to get any other accounts. You have to be satisfied with this single account for rest of your life"

Piyush pulled her closer, and looked directly into her eyes, their nose touching each other. The next moment their lips touched and they forgot the rest of the world around them. Looking at them, Armaan stood up and walked to the balcony. I walked behind him to the balcony and wrapped my right hand around his shoulder. I knew he was not sad because of them expressing their love, but because he does not have anyone in his life whom he likes the same way. I gave an assuring tap on his shoulder and said "You will get one soon"

He looked at me. He was surprised by my reaction. He turned and gave me a hug. "Am I that bad that no one likes me?" he asked

I felt my phone beep. I knew Avantika had replied. But now at this moment Armaan needed me more. So I ignored the message and instead I held his shoulders by the side, and squarely looked at his eyes, "It's because you have never looked at anyone with those emotions. The day you look at someone with love, your love will be reciprocated"

"May be you are correct. But I never found anyone attractive?"

"What kind of girl will you find attractive?"

"I am not sure. I have never thought about it"

"So do you find any of Ruchi, Neha or Akruti attractive?" I asked

"They are like sisters to me" he replied with a disgusted surprised look at me.

"Yeah I know and am not asking you to go behind them. What I am trying is to create an image of the kind of girl you like"

He thought for a moment, then said, "Sorry *yaar*, but can we not take their example?"

"Sure. You tell me if anyone comes to your mind"

"Actually no one"

"Any heroines or some movie character?" I asked

He thought for a while but then with a head movement in horizontal position conveyed to me that he was not able to relate to anyone specific.

"Hmmmm".. I thought for a while. Then said, "Let's not hurry. But you promise me, you will look at girls and try to come up with a list of what you liked in each one of them."

"And what will you get by me doing so?"

I knew he was just shy of going ahead and talking to girls, but he would never accept it. He would never accept that he has any feelings for anyone, because he thinks he will not succeed in wooing the girl and we will make fun of him. He had accepted the fact that he will get married to any girl which his parents select for him. But I feared that because he never had expressed emotions for anyone, his married life will get affected. His wife will deserve love from him, but if he didn't know how to express love, it will be difficult for their relationship to be happy. I had to bring those feelings out. "That will help you to decide on what kind of girl you like. Once we know that, we will search for such a girl for you. And when you find someone, I will help you win the girl"

He looked into my eyes. He didn't know how to react. He was happy but didn't know how to express that. He didn't know how to accept the fact that he has been long trying to get into a relationship. He just softly said "Thanks" in a hushed voice and went inside "Are you two done" he said looking at Piyush and Akruti, who were now in a much sober position.

"it's just the start" said piyush with a big blush, while Akruti slapped his back

Akruti stood up and while tying her hairs into a ponytail asked, "who all would like a tea?"

We all said a yes. Piyush turned on the TV to a football match highlights. I quietly slipped out my phone. Avantika had replied two messages

"Tell me more about the place. Will decide later whether to go out with you or not :P"

"And no public kisses. First let's get to know each other better"

I read both the messages again and again. I was relieved to know that we are still on. I was so much interested in this girl. The fact that it had been just a week of us meeting, had no impact on me. I wanted to take the relationship to the next level. I collected my thoughts and replied, "Well let's keep the details about the place secret. Just trust me on this"

"Surprise me" came the immediate response

"How about tomorrow six pm?" I enquired

Akruti came with the cups of tea in a tray. She kept my cup on the table in front of me. She sat down next to Piyush, handing him his cup. I walked over to kitchen to fetch some cookies. While I was still trying to locate the cookies, a reply came

"Office hectic nowadays. How about the next weekend?"

"Sure" I sent the message and kept the phone in pocket. I was convinced that no more messages will come today. I found the cookie box and took it to the living room. I took one and kept the box on center table. After some time me and Armaan left for my house leaving the love birds alone.

Out of Quicksand

Next Saturday I picked up Avantika from her home around noon. She was wearing a pair of white jeans with an expensive blue top. Her hairs looked different, they were fluffy and all curly. She had a nice makeup done. It looked as if I was picking her up from a parlor. She was looking amazing. She wrapped a stole covering her face and hair to save them from the air and dust while on bike. She put on big shades over her eyes. It was quite sunny, and girls across the country prefer the same precautions for face and hairs.

There was a smile on my face while I rode the bike. The effort she had put on her looks quite definitely suggested she was looking forward for this date and she wanted me to be attracted to her beauty. And sure I was. Frankly, I could never understand why girls do so much of effort on their makeup and all. What actually a boy looks are just the big eyes of his girl. He just needs her hands in his to feel the warmth of the relationship. Occasionally though, when a situation arises where the respect to the boy depends on the beauty of the girl with him, the makeup and sexy looks do come as a savior. But there is another side also to this. Girls do not understand that if they enhance their looks by make-up or appearance by cloths, the male companion is also expected to put in efforts on his looks. If he doesn't, it looks as if a beautiful princess has come out of her cozy world with a servant to take care of her needs, one who is supposed to be around her at all times. But I was at a much safe position today. Since I had been looking forward to this date, I had got myself appropriately presentable. This added to my confidence and to the smile on my face. Unlike the other day she had kept her right hand on my shoulders.

We reached a small lane and I stopped my bike below a big Gulmohar tree by a makeshift bike parking spot. The orange and red flowers were all over the road, and it looked beautiful. She stepped down the pillion, while I parked the bike in an empty slot. She removed the stole from her face, and asked me, "So!!"

I looked at her with my eyes twitched as a question. She continued, "What is the plan? And which place is this?"

Removing the helmet, I replied, "Just come along and keep expectations in check. Just one thing I can guarantee is that you will remember this day for a long time"

"Just promise me that it won't be a bad memory"

I could sense the sarcasm, but instead of laughing aloud I preferred to be more supportive. I just blinked my eyes and gave a reassuring smile. I placed my right palm by my side in a horizontal position with palm facing up. It was an invitation for her hands in mine. She looked at my palm for a second and then placed her left palm facing down on mine. She looked at me with the corner of her eyes while I tried hard to hide my smile. We started walking down the road. Gulmohar tree was planted on both side and its orange and red flowers on the road looked like a welcoming red carpet. We walked down for a few hundred meters before we turned left into a quiet small passage. This passage widened up a bit after a few steps with small window shops on either side. There were only handful customers in those shops. Further down, the density of people increased as the passage turned into a Japanese and Chinese handicraft exhibition like shops. There were cute souvenirs, hanging shades, dress materials and even knifes and martial arts related items. I didn't realize but she had slipped off her hands from mine and was busy exploring the items on sale. She was behaving as a young kid who was left alone in a room full of chocolates. She literally stopped at every shop and enquired about every object on display. She kept correlating the objects to the needs and likes of known people in her life. After some initial such stops and descriptions I had completely lost interest and was more of a robot standing behind her. By the time she was done we had over two dozen items in our shopping bags.

I looked at my watch and it was almost quarter past three. I was hungry and I badly needed a hot cup of tea. She was kind of excited and still lost in analyzing her shopping. I quietly led her to a small Tibetan food stall at the other end of the street. Finally when she sat on the plastic chair on the lane outside the stall, did she realize how hungry and thirsty she was. We quickly ordered for chicken momos and coke for her. I ordered two cups of malai tea as well for myself. The momos were fresh and yummy. Subsequently we ordered for two more plates. By the time we were done we were badly stuffed and were not in a position to get up. We decided to sit for another few minutes to gather ourselves. She was impressed by the fact that I knew the existence of such a street hidden from the main city. I knew she would like this place and was happy that she was really impressed by my choice. I wanted to show her a good time and I think she had a fair amount of it the whole afternoon.

We started walking back towards the bike when she said, "I am so full I feel like running"

"I didn't get the logic" I replied

Very innocently she replied, "When I feel tired or lethargic I try to do some intense activity to bring my energy back"

At that instant an idea crossed my mind. I couldn't stop my lips to give out a smile before I replied, "I think I have a better option than running"

"And what's that?"

"I would prefer to keep today as a day of surprises"

"The way it is going till now, I won't mind" she replied before she started giggling like a child.

I started my bike and drove through multiple dense roads before I came out in a wide residential colony road. I reached a three story brown building. It looked like any other building in the vicinity. The only difference was that this building had no visible windows on its front wall giving it a rather odd unique identity. She stepped down the bike, and asked "What place is this?"

"A place where magic happens" I replied with a mischievous smile while I removed my helmet

"And what kind of magic?" She asked with rather suspicion

"One which you cannot get over with irrespective of the number of times you feel it. Actually the more you feel it more you want it"

She narrowed her eyes on me and asked, "In literal terms or is it just your perception?"

"Just trust me" and I pulled her by her arms.

A young lady was sitting at the reception on the ground floor. She gave me a smile, "*Are* Daksh after so many days"

"Hi Ananya. Yeah the strings pulled me back. Is Eddy upstairs?"

"Yeah he is. Busy with a session"

"Ok. I will find him"

And I started climbing the stairs. Avantika closely followed me. She was clearly not comfortable. She held my hands from behind asking me to stop. "This place doesn't look like a nice place. It gives me a creepy feeling"

"Creepy?? What kind of?"

"It looks like a place where bad things happen"

"And why do you think so?"

"Its so quiet. Not even a small noise. It gives me that creepy Bollywood movie feeling"

"You mean the places where cheap sex happens?"

"Yeah. And all along this while, even you have been giving such descriptions, like magic and all"

I gave out a loud laugh. "Well it is not such kind of place. But it gives much better pleasure than what sex can give"

There was a question evident on her face. I didn't feel like explaining anything more to her and pulled her to second floor. I opened the door and let her see a group of youngsters performing salsa. She almost jumped in excitement and tears came out her eyes. She looked at me. Even though she didn't ask the question, I felt like giving an explanation to her. "This is a dance school which is run by Eddy. We as teenagers learnt a bit of Salsa dancing for a college fest dance challenge. Later I got busy with other aspects of life, Eddy made it his life."

"So you mean that you can dance?", she asked

Before I could answer, Eddy came over to us, "better than anyone else I know"

"Well this is Avantika, and Avantika this is Eddy" I said

"Hi" said Avantika

"What I can understand is that you both are trying to get into a relationship, and this boy has brought you here to impress" said Eddy with a sarcastic smile

"Nothing like that" I promptly replied while she shyly looked down and with her left hand pushed her hairs behind the left ear. "But how did you guess we are still not a couple" I told in a hushed voice into his ears

He patted my shoulders slightly and said, "It is quite evident in the nervousness you both are displaying and still she has a complete name Avantika rather than something cute"

We shared a small laugh before Eddy asked her, "So do you dance?"

"In fact I had learnt classical forms like Bharatanatayam and Kuchipudi as a young girl but have never tried a modern style like Salsa"

Before she could say anything else, I forwarded my palm asking for her hands. I walked her to the corner where we removed our shoes and led her to the dance floor. It was a wooden floor along a wall of mirror. Eddy walked over to his students on the other side of the big hall. I showed her a few steps which she tried her best to imitate. Her body was quite agile and she was quickly getting the right postures. She had a genuine grace in her steps. After around half an hour of practice, I suggested to have a dance together. She willingly accepted. The next few minutes were a bit of chaos as we both were hitting each other with hands and legs instead of dancing. We had a complete lack of coordination. Eddy was watching us from a distance. He walked over and guided us a bit for a few coordinated steps. We tried many other steps over the next hour or so, before we sat down on the floor completely tired. Inspite of the tiredness, we had a smile across our face. Eddy was also done for his day and he walked over to us. "Hope you had a nice start to salsa"

"The best start one can hope for" she replied

"You both must be tired. Let's have some tea and snacks" and we both stood up. We walked down across the road to a French café. We ordered for some puffs, biscuits and lots and lots of tea and coffee. Eddy told her about our college days where he was a year senior to me, and how we paired up for the inter college dance competition. We sat there lethargically discussing over our past and dance for another couple of hours. Eddy got a call from his wife asking about his whereabouts which prompted him to leave. And so did we.

On our ride back, she was a bit cozy on the bike. She sat close to me, her arms wrapped around me and her head resting by the back of my neck. At a traffic signal she played with the hair at back of my head poking out of the helmet. She was not able to see the smile on my face, but as a matter of fact I was very happy. She was a fun person and shared common interests. She had not tried to have an opinion about whatever we had done or talked about. I even contemplated proposing her, but the kiss on her palms had a very different reaction from her side. I didn't want to take another chance. I just kept driving. Finally we reached her house. She stepped down and stood in front of the bike. I removed my helmet and kept it on the fuel tank. She was smiling. I kept looking at her. Her smile was contagious. Even a smile swept across my face, to which she asked, "What?"

"Nothing"

"No tell me"

"I am happy to see you happy"

"That I am. I had a great day, thanks to you" and she kept her right hand over my left hands on the bike handle.

I lifted my hands, turned my palm and held her hands with fingers crossed "I am happy that you had a great day".

"I am impressed by your choice and by the fact that you know such cool places"

I gave a sheepish smile, and added "Well this is just a glimpse"

"*Ab chane ki jhaad pe mat chadho*" (now don't start boosting about yourself) she said with a naughty smile

I preferred not to react. She added, "well you can count on me any day, as now I know you have an amazing taste"

"yeah I know" I said looking directly into her eyes.

She blushed and ruffled my hairs.

A wave of confidence swept my mind. I wanted to pump up my fist in air, shout *Yippee* at peak of my voice, but I preferred to keep my emotions in check. My heart was asking me to propose her at that very instant, but my brains stopped me from doing so. Keeping the dilemma to myself, I tried to change the topic, "Hey you had some dinner plans with someone. Hope you are not late". The previous day she had told me on message that she was meeting an old friend for dinner.

She had actually completely forgotten about her plan. She quickly checked her clock. It was ten past eight. She said she needed to hurry. I also didn't feel asking more details about the friend or plans. I didn't want to project myself as interfering. So I waved a goodbye and I left for home.

I went home and ordered for a pizza for dinner. I had given the day off for my cook and Pizza was a good alternative. A nice English movie was being telecasted. I sat on the couch watching TV, but my mind was in flashback mode. The whole day was flashing back in my mind, each frame at a time. I was analyzing every moment. I didn't want to change even a single moment, other than the time when I had to leave her to have dinner with someone else. I wanted to talk to her but thinking she would be out for a dinner, I kept myself busy watching the movie.

Finally around half past ten, I sent her a message asking whether she had come back from dinner. I waited another half an hour or so before I could not stop myself from giving her a call

"Hello" came her reply. I could hear a soft music playing in the background over the phone.

"It seems you are still out" I replied

"Oh yeah. I am. Anything important Daksh?"

"No nothing urgent actually"

"Can I give you a call once I get back home?"

"Sure. Enjoy"

"Bye" she replied before she kept the call.

I felt as if I was hit by a stone right on my face. The call was short and cold. The romantic touch in her voice from earlier in the evening was amiss. I felt bad. I tried not to overthink, so kept watching TV. Slowly all channels blacked out or were taken over by teleshopping advertisements. So I switched off the TV, and picked a fictional novel and went to bed. I lay there on my elbows reading a murder thriller. I didn't realize when I dozed off.

When I woke up in the morning I saw a missed call from Avantika timed 1.20 am in the morning. She had also left me a message.

"Hey was out for long. Seems you have slept. Catch you tomorrow"

I walked over to kitchen and prepared myself butter toast and a mug of tea. I opened the Sunday times and started reading. It was not as if something new was printed, but I preferred the quiet Sunday morning where I could read the editorial and sports section in peace. While I was reading, my phone rang. It was Avantika. I had mixed emotions for her. My romantic feelings were a bit hurt by the cold call the previous night. I planned to keep a straight face while on the call,

"Hello"

"Hey Hi" she replied

"Had slept by the time you called"

"Yeah I understood it. Got a bit late"

I wanted to tell, 1.20 in the morning was not a bit late but by my standards it was super late. But since we were still not a couple officially, I checked on my words "So how was the dinner?"

"It was good. We had a nice Punjabi meal"

"Oh great. So where was it? Anyplace I know?" I was fishing for information

"We went to Taj"

"Oh wow. Taj. It must have been a special company"

"No not that special. It was just with Shobhit"

"Shobhit!!" the name sounded more of a question from my mouth

"Yeah Shobhit Taneja. My ex. Didn't I tell you about him?"

"Your Ex!!" It was a shock to me.

"Yeah we broke off around three months back. And yesterday was the first time we met post that" She must have completely missed out the shock in my voice. She kept talking with excitement.

"So was it any special occasion?" I asked sarcastically

"If we were still in a relationship, yesterday would have been our third anniversary" I was aghast listening to this nonsense. Anger was taking over me. I was angry not on her, but myself for getting interested in a girl whom I didn't know completely. Unaware of my reactions she continued "we were discussing our past and all the good days we had been together. It was fun". I was controlling my anger. She met her ex after a formal breakup on the day of anniversary. That was ridiculous. Somehow controlling my reactions I enquired, "So you two are still friends?"

"Yeah. I share everything with him?"

"Even after the break up?"

"Yeah we speak almost every day. Infact after you called me yesterday I even told him about you"

I was speechless listening to all these. I wanted to just keep the phone and never call her back. But something stopped me from doing so. May be it was Shubho's words. He had warned me that I should face these challenges rather than run away on slightest hints of trouble. I wanted to see how bad this can get. While I was lost in my thoughts, she continued "He wants to meet you as well. How about next weekend?"

"And why should I meet him?"

"I think you two will make good friends"

Here I was trying to win this girl, and this girl was asking me to befriend her ex. I was ridiculed by the thought. I snapped "No I don't think we will"

"Now don't respond like this. Keep your male ego at bay."

"Its not about male ego. Its about being logical. Maintaining friendship with an ex is just ridiculous. That shows you are still not out of a relationship. You still have feelings"

"No it is no like that. It shows maturity of a person"

"Could be, but I don't think I am too liberal with these thoughts"

"Now don't make this an issue out of proportion" she snapped

"Well I am not trying to. Anyway I have some urgent work. I will call you later" I tried to get away from this conversation.

"Ok. Take your time"

"Bye" and I hanged up the call.

I sat there trying to absorb the facts she shared with me. I looked up and shouted, "GOD!! Why you always pick me for these shit", and I walked to the washbasin and poured cold water on my head and face. I called up Armaan and we planned to meet for Lunch.

The rest of the day I was trying to not think about Avantika. She messaged me twice but I preferred to ignore her messages. In the evening I went to the lake and sat by the stone. I wanted some ME time. I was lost in my thoughts when my mother called

"*Hain* Maa" (Tell me, mother)

"How are you?"

"I am good Maa. How are you and Baba?"

"You don't seem to be good" I don't know how mothers get to know when something is wrong. Well I didn't say anything, and would never share these issues with her. I tried to change the topic, "Uff Maa. Everything is fine."

"Ok. If you say so. I called up to remind you that you need to call Disha"

I had given Avantika a try and at that moment I was really pissed off at her. I didn't see a reason why I should not give my parents' choice also a fair chance, and at that moment Disha sounded a good distraction from all this fuzz. "Yes Maa. Give me an hour. I will reach home and give her a call."

"Are you sure you will? Or is it just another instance where you push away this serious topic?"

I could feel the pain in her voice. "No Maa. I am definitely calling her today"

My mother was happy to hear that. After a few more questions about my health and work we hanged up the call. Even it was getting dark, and I left back for home.

On reaching home, I took a bath and then a cup of tea while I mentally prepared myself to give a call to Disha. Finally I picked up my phone. I was trying to do something which I had been avoiding for so long for so many reasons. I dialed the number

"Hello"

"Hi!! Is this Disha?"

"Yes. And whom I am talking to?"

Well Well Well. That was one sweet voice. And it was a voice of a confident person. I liked it straight away. "This is Daksh here"

"Daksh!!" she sounded as a question "Do I know you?"

"Well I think you would remember the young kid with long hairs who smashed all your dolls some fifteen years back"

"Is it the same one whom my parents called an evil when he did that, but are now trying to patch me up for life saying him to be a changed gentleman"

"Yeah I think so, I am the same guy"

"So do you still have the long hairs and do you still trouble other girls and their toys?" she asked with a smile in her voice

"Well age took away the best of me. Now I am just another face. My talents left me"

She smiled on my sarcasm. "So what are you upto these days?"

"Nothing much. Just a boring job. What about you?"

"Same here"

There was a silence for a few moments, both searching for words. Finally she spoke "So what prompted you to the idea of getting married?"

"Actually it is not me. But its my mother who thinks I should get married, and that you are the perfect one"

"well my mother also has something similar to tell about you and marriage"

"What is your take on this?" I asked

"Marriage or you?"

"Well I meant marriage, but if you have an opinion about me too, I would be interested to know that as well"

"Frankly speaking I don't think I am ready to get married. And getting married to a person whom I am not familiar with is quite difficult. Nothing against you but had expected to first know you better before I can comment on whether we should get married or not. What do you say?"

"Well I do second your thoughts. I also think we should get to know each other first before our parents finalize something"

"Well we can consider this call as a starting point"

I was impressed by her confidence and frankness. "Yeah. Well now you have my number as well, do give me a call whenever you feel like"

"Sure I can, but don't you have work to do. What if I call when you are busy at office?"

"I hope that will be an urgent one. Otherwise I believe you also have an office to attend to"

She laughed aloud. I was happy to hear that, but frankly I was not in a mood for a long talk. I was never comfortable getting introduced to a person on phone. It was as if talking to a person without a face. It was as if she was able to hear my mind. She replied, "I have some plans for the night, and I am getting late for it. If you don't mind can we talk later?"

I tried to show some disappointment in my voice, "Oh ok. Sure. Have a nice evening"

"That I will. Bye"

"Bye"

We hung up the call. I had a missed call from Avantika and a message asking me to call her back. I was frankly not in a mood to talk to her. It was also the time of my cook to show up. So I decided to call her post dinner and let her know by a message.

Later in the night I gave her a call

"Hello"

"So how are you?" I asked straightaway

"Why are you acting so differently?"

"I think you know the reason"

"No I don't. I will prefer you explain it to me"

"Do I need to. Isn't it evident?"

"No it is not"

"Well I think you are aware that I have some feelings for you"

"Yes I know that. But is that a problem?"

"The problem is that you are still in a very close friendship with your ex"

"So what is the problem with it? He is a nice person and I like hanging out with him."

"Well I won't consider that to be a welcome expectation from a person of my liking"

"Ufff…. You males have so much of ego issues"

"It is not an issue about ego. It is more of a normal human logic"

"You meet him once and then I will ask you about logic"

"But when you still like talking to each other why did you break up at first place?"

"Because we knew his family will never accept me, and hence we called off our relationship. But that doesn't mean I stop liking him as a close friend"

Somehow I could not correlate to this logic. Someone may call it conservative, but friendship post a broken relationship never made sense to me. Anger was taking over me for being interested in this girl and still listening to all this nonsense. It was not acceptable to me. Breakup seemed an intelligent thing to do, but Shubho's words kept coming back to me.

"May be we should talk later on this. I don't seem to be in a good mood"

"Ok. If you say so, we will talk later"

After we hanged up I went out for a walk. It was one of the longest walks.

I did try

Over the next week, I shuffled calls and messages between Avantika and Disha. My heart was still willing to go for Avantika, but my mind was completely against her. On the other hand my heart was still against Disha, and my head still confused about her and the circumstances under which we had been introduced. Inside I was burning with the feeling of infidelity. On a few days I even had the urge to stop interacting with either of them. But then my heart wanted not to. I was actually confused.

During our interactions, Disha had invited me to Mumbai for a formal meet and know each other better. I tried to postpone it as much as possible as my heart was still wooing for Avantika. I wanted her in my life, I wanted the issues between us to get resolved. For me a formal meeting with Disha was a last resort in case the situation with Avantika didn't materialize.

Avantika on other hand kept asking me to meet and befriend Shobhit. She was to meet him again for a dinner on Sunday at Novel park restaurant. She had asked me also to come. This was a garden restaurant by the highway. I didn't understand the need to meet. I kept persuading her not to meet her ex for another time, but she was adamant on getting me befriended with him. It was a very irritating scenario. I thought of sharing this development with Shubho, Arpit, Armaan or Piyush and take their advice. But it was my fight with my internal feelings. And I wanted my inner self to find its own solution. Though having dinner with her ex was completely un-acceptable for me, but deep inside I did want to see the two ex-love birds interacting before I make my mind.

Finally the Sunday arrived. Avantika called me early in the morning reminding me for the dinner. I formally again rejected the offer. But she said she would be expecting me before we hanged up the call. I preferred to spend my whole day playing Call of Duty. While playing a sniper shot, I got an idea. Late in the evening I drove down to Novel Park and parked in a dark alley just outside the restaurant. I searched for a corner from where I could see them but they could not. Avantika was sitting next to a well-built person in a blue half jacket. I could see him only waist up. He had short hairs, but a long knot at the back of his head like the ancient Hindu Brahmins. He had a dragon tattoo on his right bicep and a pair of metallic rings on his left wrist. He was wearing a wrist watch with red band and a white pair of spectacles. It seemed as if his identity depended on these small distinguished stuffs. She had told me that he had tried his luck twice unsuccessfully in business ventures and at present was organizing funds for his next venture. She had a constant smile on her face, which clearly showed she enjoyed his company. He on the other hand was not leaving even a single chance to touch her. A possessive shine was evident in his eyes. There was no doubt that he was still in love with her and all this was another chance to get her back in his life. It seemed as if she was the biggest achievement in his life and he could not let it slip off his hands.

I had my answer. I didn't want to get in between both of them. They were very much in love, just that they were trying hard to ignore the fact. I had no future with her. It would have been just a matter of time when she would have realized her mistake in a relationship with me. I had no time and energy to put into a relationship which I knew had no destination. I had been through a lot in my past and I just didn't want another bad experience. I walked back to my bike, started it and off I went. Middleway on my way home, I changed my mind and instead drove to Armaan's house.

Later in the night Arpit called and updated us with the news that his marriage date had been finalized. It was scheduled just three weeks later at Varanasi and a post marriage reception at Bengaluru. It was indeed news to be celebrated and we drove down to Arpit's house. Neha, Shubho, Ruchi, Piyush and Akruti were already there. We had a small party till early morning. Avantika had called a couple of times but she was already in my blocked list. I had earlier sent her a message saying we had different destinations in life and we should keep continuing our own journey. I preferred to break off my perusal for her, in a message as I didn't know how to explain the reason behind my extreme step. In our earlier conversations she was not even ready to acknowledge the issue.

Next evening I was booking six flight tickets to Varanasi. I had been given the responsibility to book the tickets for the gang. Arpit and Neha were scheduled to travel early. Our parents were coming directly from our home town. I had made my mind about Avantika, I was rather in peace. And

Arpit Neha's marriage was just the perfectly timed opportunity for me to focus on something else. My phone beeped for a message. It was from Disha. As per my mother's advice I had to seriously give Disha's proposal a try. She had been constantly inviting me to Mumbai. As I was already booking tickets, I thought of finally booking a ticket to Mumbai as well. I called her up and confirmed if we could meet the next weekend. As she was fine with the plan, I booked a flight to Mumbai for the coming Friday evening.

In the night after I was done with my dinner, Ruchi gave me a call. Avantika had called her up and told her about my sudden change in behavior. She expected Ruchi's intervention to bring things back on track

"Heard that you are not taking her calls and not even replying to the messages" she asked

"Yes." I was not in a mood to speak on that topic, hence preferred to keep my answers short

"And why so?"

"Ask her"

"No I am asking you"

"I actually don't want to have a relationship with her. And hence I am trying to avoid any bigger complication which may arise in coming days"

"But didn't you like her?"

I did think for a moment before replying, "I was definitely attracted to her. And I do not deny that. But unless and until you get to know a person, you cannot fall in love with her. We have different destinations in life and we know that even before we have the chance to know each other completely."

"Why what happened? Why are you talking about extremes?"

I knew she would keep pushing till she knew everything. So I told her the whole story about Shobhit. Avantika had not told her anything about him and that complicated angle. Ruchi was also in shock when I told her about closeness with her ex. She also had the same opinion that it would lead to major complications later in the relationship. She backed my decision and assured me that she will convey my decision about the relationship to her. Also she would try to explain her this point of view which she is not ready to accept.

Over the next couple of days I did get a few emotional messages from Avantika and a few offending messages from Shobhit. I preferred not to reply back to his messages. I was happy and content with my decision. I did reply back to Avantika,

"You are a great person and anyone will be happy to be in your life. But knowing myself well, I know that the person will not be me. I have different expectations in life, and I would still prefer to pursue them. Take care"

She never replied back.

-x-

Next Friday I left office early for airport. I had called Jatin in the morning to let him know about my Mumbai visit. We used to be roommates in college. After graduation he had joined a Stock Broking company in Mumbai and had placed himself in a good position. All these years after college, we had been in touch over phone but never had a chance to meet. I was planning to stay with him during my Mumbai visit. I was anxiously looking ahead to catch up with him after all those years.

I was travelling to Mumbai with a mixed feeling. It was the first time that my parents had selected a girl for me and asked me to get familiarized. Over the last couple of weeks we were in constant touch over phone. But other than her pleasing voice I had found very little common in her and my expectations. She was more of a dreamer and I had always looked for someone more grounded. She always insisted for a face to face interaction. Even my parents shared the same opinion. And there I was catching a flight to Mumbai, to meet her. I was travelling with an expectation to get to know her better in person. After my security check was done, I called her. She had made plans to meet the next evening. She was taking coaching classes for CAT, and hence she was unable to make earlier plans in the day. And frankly I was fine with it. Somewhere deep within me, I was more excited to meet Jatin rather than Disha on my Mumbai visit.

After calling Disha, I called up Jatin. He was still in office. Though he had promised in morning that he would pick me up from airport, he expressed his inability to do so as some sudden work pressure had come in. He asked me to take a taxi to his home. After the call he messaged me his home address.

The flight was short and as I stepped out of flight in Mumbai, I was greeted with the cool sea breeze. I walked down to the pre-paid taxi counter and booked myself a cab. Jatin had warned me about the *taxiwalas* of Mumbai, and hence a reputed pre-paid service was the only intelligent option for a person like me who was making his debut visit to a mega metro city named Mumbai. I had been warned of such horrific stories about the taxi wallas and local goons, that I sat quietly in the taxi with my fingers crossed. All the way, inspite of the taxi being pre-paid I felt I was being driven in a longer route. At a stretch which was lonely and dark, I literally paralyzed and repeatedly recited *maha mrityunjay jaap*. Finally after an hour and half I reached Shriram apartments. I was so excited to finally meet Jatin after so many years. So many memories were flashing across my mind. I took the lift up to the sixth floor and after pressing the door-bell I started tapping the door with the signature drum beats we used to do during our college days.

A few moments later the door was opened by a beautiful girl dressed in spaghetti

and a pair of shorts. Her hairs were tied in a ponytail. She gave me the coldest stare I had ever received. I knew Jatin used to live alone, so I got defensive and I blurted out "I thought it is my friends house"

"So does that mean you will tap the door as if there was no tomorrow?"

"Actually that beat was our college trademark. But sorry I disturbed you at this hour"

She narrowed her eyes on me. More than the spine chill I was getting by the stare, I was more interested to meet Jatin. So I asked, "Do you know which door Jatin lives in?"

Her stare gave way to a cute smile, "Are you Daksh?"

I had a confused look on my face, "Yes I am. But how do you know me?"

"I am Gargi. Jatin and me live together. He told me about you, but I was not expecting you for another hour"

She opened the door completely and waved me to come in. She continued, "Jatin is still not home. He should be here any minute now"

I was completely feeling awkward. I didn't know how to react. Jatin had never told me about Gargi. I didn't know what their relationship status is and how should I react to all these. I placed my bag by the sofa and awkwardly spoke "Well I didn't know you both stay together. Otherwise I would have stayed in a hotel"

"Why so. No need to be so formal. You both were roommates for so many years in college. Jatin has told me so much about you. I am happy to finally see the face to the most talked about character in this house"

I wanted to say that Jatin had never spoken about you, but I preferred to wait for Jatin to come and formally introduce us to each other. "Well that's so nice of you. Hope I will not be much of a trouble"

She laughed out loud, "this formality doesn't match the picture portrayed about you in my head"

I felt another punch of awkwardness. I preferred to give a subtle smile. She instead brought me a glass of water. I was standing all this while. She waved her hands in a motion to ask me to sit. I placed myself to the corner single couch. "I didn't mean to offend your peace with that door tap"

"Uff... No need to be so formal. That's OK"

There was a couple of moments of silence before she said, "I was in middle of an office task. If you won't mind can I just finish that off?"

"Please go ahead. I don't want to interrupt you", I said while picking up a magazine from the side table.

She went inside. A few minutes later the door-bell rang. I knew it had to be Jatin and I wanted to finally meet the known face I had been expecting. But I preferred to sit while Gargi rushed to open the door. As the door opened, they both shared a quick kiss. Finally it was Jatin. I stood up from my couch but my feet were frozen. Jatin had put on weight, was flashing a beard and was dressed in a suit. He rushed to me and we shared a long hug.

Finally he spoke, "You haven't changed a bit"

"But you have become more human"

He instantly knew I was talking about his suit. He literally lived all four years of college in a single pair of jeans and a t-shirt. "Sometimes you need to degrade to fit in the company"

"So how is work going? And how is life?"

"All are fine. You have already met Gargi. We live together."

"When did this happen? Don't tell me you are married"

He laughed out, "If we were we would have definitely sent you an invitation. Either for marriage, or for being a witness in registrar's office." Gargi brought a glass of water for him and sat by his side on the couch. "We met around two years back when she came to our office for financial planning. The moment I saw her, I was head over heels. I made sure I take up her case. In a few months I definitely proved my mettle in handling finances for her and she was impressed by my skills. That is where we started"

They both had wrapped their arms across each other and had a constant smile on their lips. "So when did this happen" I asked waving my hands showing the house

"We know we have to get married, so we moved in together. May be very soon we will get married"

"But you never told us"

"That's because our parents have a few inhibitions and they themselves don't know about our little arrangement here. So we thought of telling everyone once things are sorted out at our home front"

I gave back an assuring smile "things will turn out to be good"

"Why don't you freshen up? Then we can have dinner" he suggested.

He picked my bag and walked me to the guest bedroom. The house was very neat and very well maintained. I quickly freshened up in the attached bathroom but was caught in a dilemma. I had brought just boxers as I was not aware of Gargi's presence in the house. So I wore the same jeans and put on a cotton t shirt. The dinner was delicious. Post dinner we sat in the balcony floor with our legs hanging down through the grill. We were talking about our college days and Gargi was intently listening to our conversation. But soon she drifted off in a sleep. Jatin pulled her up in his arms and carried her to bed. He came back and we continued talking over cups of coffee. We finally went to bed around four am. Jatin slept with me in the guest room.

Early morning I woke up with a heavy bladder. Jatin was not in the bed. Instead I could hear love making sounds from the next room. This was a first to me. I didn't know how to respond to this situation. I preferred to keep my eyes shut and pretend to sleep. My bladder immediately needed a leak but I held on with my act. The next few minutes seemed like hours. The sounds turned to giggling and back to love making. I held on my act through all these. But finally I had to prioritize nature's call. When I came out of the toilet, Jatin was standing there. "Hope you had a nice sleep"

"I did" I replied

"So how about French toast as breakfast?"

"Sounds yummee"

Behind him Gargi walked to kitchen tying her hairs into a ponytail. We sat down on the couch and switched on the TV. He walked back to the kitchen to prepare tea. I preferred to leave them alone, as already I had woken up to awkwardness.

In breakfast table, Jatin asked me, "So what brought you to Mumbai?"

I hadn't told him about Disha earlier and I had no inhibitions of hiding the facts from him. "Actually my parents are pushing me to get married to a girl. So I am here to meet her in person and decide on my own"

"Wow that's surprising"

"What is surprising?"

"A person like you planning to get married to a girl chosen by parents"

"I am not getting married straight away. I am here to meet. Decision will be taken much later once I know her better. It may be negative"

"Mark my words, my dear boy. The Casanova has lost the touch."

"And who is that?"

Gargi jumped in, "we all know who that is"

The morning was fun. Jatin had taken the day off. We had lunch in a nice restaurant. It was nice to meet Jatin and to know Gargi. They were definitely in love and perfect for each other. They were in sync on everything.

Later in the evening I took a taxi to Ville Parle. I was dressed in a gray suit and a blue shirt. As I had never formally met anyone for a marriage introduction date, my mother had suggested me to go in a very formal wear and be very formal. She kept on reminding me that I was carrying the family's reputation and family upbringing and values on my shoulders. She wanted me to make a lasting impression on Disha. I personally would have preferred a much casual dress but since I had come down to Mumbai just to please my mother, I had planned to follow her suggestions as well.

Disha had planned to meet me near Ville Parle. Since I was new to the city she thought it will be easy on me to locate a major landmark like the Ville Parle station. I reached there a few minutes before seven and stood in front of what looked like a decent mobile phone store. I tried to call Disha to know her exact location but she didn't answer my calls. It was around quarter past seven she called me up. She asked me my exact location and the dress I was wearing. Some while later a red car stopped next to me. From inside a middle aged male looked out and asked if I was looking for someone. I preferred not to respond. The man turned out to be a pimp and kept trying to make a hard sale. In the meantime another blue car came and stopped just behind this car. It kept flickering the headlight and kept honking till the red car left. This car came forward and stopped next to me. The tinted window rolled down and I could see a girl in a short bright outfit and an overly done makeup. I straightaway motioned my hands asking the lady to go ahead. I was feeling ashamed to be standing at an improper stop. The lady instead kept asking something but her words got lost in the noise of the traffic. Finally I bent over to the height of the window. She was asking, "Are you Daksh?"

In a flash I figured out that she was Disha. "Disha?" I asked

"Yes. Exactly. Now hop in. I am already stopping an angry traffic"

I hopped in. The car smelled sweet. But the smell was overpowered by the smell of perfume she had worn. Her dress was definitely very short. Her shapely thighs were bare, but my eyes stopped at the big cleavage. She looked more vulgar than hot. I was very uncomfortable. Not even in my dreams, I expected her to turn up in such a dress. Lost in my thoughts, she tried to start a conversation

"Hope you didn't have difficulty finding the place"

"No not exactly"

"So how is Mumbai treating you?"

"Still need to be treated. So where are we going?"

"There is a nice place nearby in Juhu. It has the best parties. Lets go there"

I had actually expected a nice quieter place where we could sit and talk to know each other better. But just keeping the tempo high, I nodded in affirmative.

"But you are in a suit. How would you look inside?" she added

"Why what's the problem in the dress"

"It is more of a young crowd who dress rather casually"

I looked at myself. I had an idea. "Leave that to me. I will gel inside"

She stared at me but didn't speak another word. She drove to a place named "Piccasso's". The valet was quite familiar to her. She handed over her keys while we stepped in. The big bouncer standing at the entrance gave her a big smile, "Hey DG the gang is already here" he said.

DG? I thought. It came down to me that it must be the short form of her name *Disha Ghatak.* But what is the gang? And how does everyone know her around? I preferred to wait and watch. On the right side was a coat room where I deposited my coat. My blue shirt was rather bright and it gelled well in the crowd. The crowd was very young. All girls were in revealing short dresses while the boys were in t-shirts and tight jeans. A group of four boys and two girls came rushing towards us. One of the boys picked Disha up in her arms. Another one gave her a long hug. They all looked very close friends. The other girls were also wearing similar kind of provoking dress. Disha introduced them to me. In the loud music I actually couldn't

make out their names. But it seemed like they all knew about me and the party was a planned activity. I was feeling awkward. Attending a dance party with her crazy friends was definitely not what I had thought about my first date with her.

In a few minutes we were dancing to some cool music. They had some crazy steps but most of them were creepy. They danced very close to each other. Slowly the movements became a little vulgar. The boys were literally hovering over the girls. I was feeling ashamed with their dance moves. They had completely forgotten about me. What I felt the most was that Disha was also more into her friends rather than being with me. I had flown a thousand miles to come and meet her so that we could formally get to know each other better. And instead she had brought me to a party where it was very difficult to talk, and then completely forgotten about me. My mother had described her as a soft spoken homely girl, but I was seeing her in a short sleazy dress making some vulgar dance moves. For our generation the party and dance was fine but keeping a dual identity with parents and another for friends had never been my kind of thing. I was pissed off. It did occur to me that she may be doing this deliberately, so that I call off the marriage talks and become the one to be blamed by parents.

Keeping my emotions in check I tried to give another try to talk to her. I moved closer and asked her to step out of dance floor so that we can talk a bit. But she completely ignored me. That reaction in which she turned back to dance with her friends, snapped something inside me. I picked up my coat and walked outside. I called up a taxi and gave Jatin's address in Navi Mumbai. Inspite of me phobic to the taxis of Mumbai, I sat in one not bothering about the route or the driver. I was thinking about the bad experience I had and what I would say to my mother. I picked up my phone and typed a message to Disha

"Thanks for the invitation to Mumbai. I liked the city but not its people. Enjoy your party. And tell your parents the marriage will never happen as the boy is out of your league."

I reached Jatin's home. I had a very uncomfortable and angry look on my face. Jatin straight away knew something was wrong. I told him and Gargi the complete story on how my parents were pushing me for this girl. How they had made such an ideal cultured girl image of her in my mind, and how she turned up today. They backed my decision to walk out on her. I felt good to have the support. We had a quick dinner. Later we again sat on the balcony. Earlier I had kept my Sunday reserved for Disha, but now I was free. Jatin suggested going to Khandala and Lonavla on a drive, and we all liked the idea. We planned to leave early the next day and everyone went to sleep.

I lay there on the bed on my back looking blankly at the ceiling. I was trying to figure out how to put the facts in front of mom. I knew she won't believe me and she would consider it my attempt to run away from marriage. A smile of desperation ran across my lips. I wanted to be in a relationship, one who wanted to settle down, but the irony of life was to come across such people who looked like prospective milestones but were rather just a pit-stop. I had to blame myself also for that, but I always felt that I deserved someone better. I liked most of them but could fall in love only with Alia. The more I knew each one of them, the more I turned away. I wish I could settle for anyone, but I just wanted a decent one who loved live as it is. One who is simple, smart and sweet. I was back at square zero with both Avantika and Disha out of the scene. I had to make a fresh start but deep within I didn't want to. I had run a lot searching for the perfect one. I was tired of running. I wanted some rest. My father always says, leave it to destiny. I never believed that concept, but that day I wanted to.

Next morning we went for the drive. Around noon, Disha called. I preferred not to pick her call. She tried a couple of more times. Finally she dropped me a message

"Hey didn't notice you had left. Saw your message now only. I am sorry if I was too involved with my friends and couldn't give you more time. Lets meet today at a place of your choice"

I didn't reply to her message. Instead I added her number to my blocked call list.

I took the late night flight back to Bengaluru. On reaching Bengaluru I straight away went to office. The day was hectic and could only find time to call home late in the night. I told mom everything that happened about Disha. She was not ready to believe my words. She had that cultured soft spoken homely girl image of Disha in her mind. She kept blaming me for making stories about her. I didn't know how to convince her. So I asked her to talk to *mamaji*, Disha's neighbors. On saying this she somehow trusted everything I told her earlier. I could never understand mothers. She instead changed her track to how will I ever find a girl given my limited education (bengali's still consider a graduate partially educated), limited looks, less salary and the fact that I lived outside Kolkata. I didn't bother to reply as I knew all my words will fall into deaf ears. She was getting hyper. Dad took the receiver from her. I still remember his words. He had said, "Marriage is an institution and you will never find the exact one you are looking for. Rather you will find one who will somehow fit your criteria list after a few iterations of modifications and editing. And your inner self will be okay to settle down with this person. Then both of you will work together for years to make your marriage work through rough and bright patches to make the marriage the perfect one". The words sounded more of a defeatist approach to marriage. I wanted to marry the one who fits perfectly to my search criteria and no one else. But then what my father told me was more about the truth of life. There could be a perfect match for everyone in world but it is very difficult for everyone to search for that one in this big world with such huge population. Instead most people find the first decent and the closest one to their criteria, and settle down happily. Only a few lucky ones get the perfect one. My search for the perfect one had yet not materialized and I was slowly becoming the part of the majority.

I didn't want to think of my marriage or the perfect one for some time and I told my parents also about this. They were okay with my decision, but I knew they would not sit idle.

Armaan's roller coaster ride

It was the auspicious evening of Arpit's post marriage reception in Bengaluru. He had organized a grand reception at the Taj. Everyone looked happy, and needless to say, Arpit and Neha were the happiest. Their relationship was finally cemented by the sacred ritual of marriage. And this sacred term had brought a lot of changes in them over the past couple of days. With the feeling of marriage getting absorbed in them, Neha had mellowed down a bit and was seen less controlling of Arpit. It was a big change. For us who knew them so close, it was infact a huge change. Arpit had also suddenly gained confidence and he looked like a man in control. We were all happy for them.

Armaan and me stood at the corner near the entrance. We two bachelors felt lonely in the gathering. We only had each other's company. We had nothing constructive to do and slowly we found ourselves browsing the crowd for pretty faces and discussing our opinions. There were a few faces which were distinctly standing out. One of them was a girl draped in a silver saree. She was excessive talkative. She was attracting some attention but mostly glares. She was a college friend of Neha. She was excited for her friend's marriage, and had taken too much of liquor. We had some funniest one liners to share about her. We felt that the attention she was getting was driving further her craziness.

We could see Shubho and Ruchi happily dancing to the soft music on the dance floor. They were indeed a perfect couple and they complemented each other well in every aspect. We were searching for Piyush and Akruti but couldn't find them. Instead they spotted us. They walked over to us. Piyush had his hands wrapped around her shoulder. The love birds couldn't keep their hands off each other. They even could not walk as two separate humans. As soon as they arrived to our strategic location, Akruti pointed in a certain direction and spoke, "Stop getting distracted by that hyper. You are missing on the girl to your eight o'clock draped in a red saree."

We turned that way. She was tall, with straight hair and drop dead gorgeous. But to me she didn't look cute, and my eyes wandered again to her friends and then back to others. Akruti was game and she shifted my attention towards the one in a cute pink frock. Her dress was definitely cute but she was not. Even Piyush jumped into the fishing game and kept suggesting me the selected ones. While we kept fishing for pretty girls from our spot, Shubho and Ruchi came inviting us to the dance floor. It was indeed a happy day and we couldn't miss to dance. We went ahead towards the center of the hall for a dance. It was then we realized that Armaan wasn't with us. He was still standing in that corner near the entrance with his head turned towards the gorgeous girl in red saree. He was literally mesmerized by that girl. His head followed every move by the girl. We all walked down to him and quietly stood behind watching his reactions. He was un-aware of our presence. He was actually un-aware of the party and the hundreds of people around him. He was in his own world.

We watched him for a few more minutes ogling at that girl. It was as if he was dreaming with open eyes. Piyush held his shoulders square from back and gave him a sudden push. The glass in his hand fell and its broken pieces scattered all over. The sudden noise made many heads turn towards us, but soon they turned back to the food and conversations they were enjoying. A housekeeping boy quickly came and cleaned up the mess. Armaan stood there facing us still lost in some dream.

"Hey Armaan what happened?" I asked

"I don't think he is in his senses" Ruchi said

"Splash water on his face" came the idea from Shubho

"*Do chapet maar saale ko*"(slap him couple of times) was Piyush's idea.

Finally Armaan's eyes looked at us and he spoke, "She is the one. Man she is the most gorgeous women I have ever seen"

"The one in red saree?" Akruti asked

"Oh my god. She is so beautiful" Armaan kept blabbering in his own world.

We had never seen him like this. He was always the one with the funny one liners about girls and couples. We had never known him to have any emotions for a girl. We knew he was not gay, but at times we did doubt him for being straight. He was finally showing some emotions for a girl. Me and Piyush wrapped around his arms walked him over to the rest room. He was still not in his senses. We filled the basin with water and immersed his head into it repeatedly. An old guest who came by to take a leak, looked suspiciously at us, but he knew we were not trying to kill him by drowning his head under water. Finally Armaan came to his senses. He sat down below the blower with his elbows on his knee and hands on his hair.

"Hey Armaan, what happened man?" Piyush asked

"I don't know. All of a sudden my vision got fuzzy. I could see nothing but that girl in red saree. She was all I could see."

I couldn't hide a smile "It happens to everyone someday or other" I tried to sound assuring

"It has never happened to me" Armaan said

"Man he is in love" said Piyush.

"Don't tell me this is love" he protested

"This is just the first step. Love makes you forget the rest of the world but just that person. And that is what happened here. Don't you ever watch Hindi movies" asked Piyush

"Never the romantic ones"

"Don't worry. You will get used to this" and we burst out in laughter.

"But I don't even know her name, I don't know anything about her. I don't know what to do next?"

"Don't worry man. We have BABA with us" said Piyush. After him getting into a relationship with Akruti, he had started calling me BABA. I was looked up as the Love Guru of the gang. But I knew deep inside I was not. I had just used common sense in his case. Both of them had their eyes on me.

"Lets act normal and get back to the party. We will see what we can do" I said. Armaan quickly dried up his face and combed his hairs. We walked out to Shubho and Ruchi. In the meanwhile, Akruti had walked over to that girl in red saree and we could see them talking. When she came back, she declared "Her name is Snigdha Menon, and she works with Neha. She lives in Kormangala. This is all what I could get"

I shared a high five with her. She was definitely cool. She knew Armaan would be looking for details and while we were inside bringing him back to senses, she had done the homework. We made sure the rest of our party was around Armaan and Snigdha. We got the official photographer click some splendid photographs of her. In one photo we even managed to get both of them in a single frame. I know it was childish, but it was fun.

The party finally ended and guests left. We were the last ones in the hall. Arpit and Neha had been busy the whole evening to pose for snaps with the guests and as the hosts. They didn't get time to eat anything and they were hungry as ever. We had made sure to keep aside the best of the dishes for them. They were busy gorging on the food when we broke the news of *Pehla nasha pehla Pyaar* (love at

first sight) of Armaan for Snigdha. It was a shock even to them. Picturing Armaan with a girl was indeed a distant imagination for all of us. Neha warned us that she was a pretty happening girl in office and at all times was surrounded with friends and fans. Boys do crazy stuff in office to get her attention, but she knows how to handle them at a distance. But this was Armaan's first love and we all were going to stand for him. We had to make it work. We took oaths of friendship and painted a happy romantic future for Armaan. A lot of fun later, we all left for our homes.

Armaan came with me to my house. Piyush dropped Akruti to her home and joined us. We had just one topic to discuss that night. We made a bit of fun of Armaan's reactions in the party. We imitated him, and even he found it funny. He still couldn't understand why he reacted that way in the party. He was in a much better state now once Snigdha was not around. A while later we all sat seriously to discuss and find a way by which Armaan could win her. According to Neha's description about her, it was very clear that she was used to get a lot of attention from boys. We were quite sure she must have been proposed a multiple times as well. As a fact, Armaan was not handsome like Brad Pitt, and we knew for sure that no girl will feel weak in the knees for his looks. There was a possibility of Neha introducing him to her, but doing that he will just be one of the thousand faces around her. Also looking at Armaan's reaction earlier that day we were confident that he could not just walk over and get himself introduced and make an impression with his wit and one liners. We feared he will just forget everything and make a complete fool of himself while he would be standing there unaware of his deep stare.

Even after a lot of deliberations, we were unable to find a concrete idea for a perfect introduction. The fact that we knew very less about her was also hindering our planning process. We wished walking over to a girl and getting introduced was a simple task. But the truth is that it is just a single chance. If we screw up that chance or don't make a lasting impression, we usually close all doors for that to happen again.

After a lot of thinking, the best we could suggest him was to observe her a few days from a distance. That in no way meant stalking, but it meant to do a complete and rigorous homework before going for the final kill. We even planned to take Neha's help for the same.

Neha was a sport and she was with us in this plan. Over the next few days, Armaan in the pretext of picking up Neha from office, kept an eye on Snigdha. In the few days to follow he was very much aware of her office timings and weekly schedules. He also knew her residence and everything about all the girls she lived with. He even got introduced to couple of them. Living with us he had learned over years that one of the easiest ways to get introduced to a girl is through her friends. But he had no courage to use them as a ladder. Another quite evident thing which he observed was that she was always on phone.

He was completely disheartened about the fact that she was always on phone with someone. On an optimistic front I suggested that it was possible that she was not always speaking to the same person on the other side of the call. It could be that she was in calls with her mother or her family or her friends. But he was pretty convinced that she was in call with her boyfriend. But inspite of this doubt, he was head over heels for her. He found her to be perfect. But we had to know more about her. We had to know her as a friend. We were still trying to figure out a way to get him introduced. Armaan was also convinced that she knew that he has been following her and that he was interested in her. He couldn't understand why we were taking such elaborate steps for the planning. He just wanted to walk over to her and open up his heart.

In the meantime Akruti found that his colleague Akash was a college friend of Snigdha and they still hang out sometimes. On a pretext of a small get together at her house she got Armaan and me introduced to Akash. Over the next few weeks, we made sure to have Akash as a constant part of our weekend plans. Finally the day arrived which we had been waiting for. It was Akash's birthday and only limited friends were invited to his house. He had invited us and Snigdha as well. Initially Armaan was nervous, but then I walked over to her,

"I think I know you from somewhere"

"That's a very old pick up line" she smiled back

"Who said I am interested in you. I don't think you are my type"

She was actually taken aback. She didn't expect such an answer. I think no one had ever given her such an answer. "But I don't remember you"

I faked it but said, "Were you there in Arpit and Neha's marriage reception?"

"Yes I was. But how do you know Neha?"

"Aah!! That's where I think I have seen you. Small World you see. Arpit is my buddy"

"Oh"

I continued, "Actually we are a gang of friends and Neha joined us to get acquainted with Arpit"

She laughed. I continued, "Everyone is special in some way in our gang"

"And what is your speciality?" she asked

"I specialize in talking nonsense. Well the smart and the witty one is Armaan" at which point I pulled Armaan by his arms. "And he is Armaan"

"Hi" said Armaan

"He says you are the wit expert. So where did you get it from?" she asked him

"The same place where people forget it" he mumbled slowly with his eyes looking down.

Clearly he was feeling shy and nervous in front of her. Even though he was almost inaudible, she did hear it, and she smiled "nice one"

Her smile actually acted as a morale booster for him. Over the next few minutes, he was back to his witty best. As they were enjoying each other's company, I left them alone and got myself busy interacting with other guests. They both were inseparable the rest of the evening. They even shared numbers. Armaan came back to my home for the night. He was in a good mood and could not believe his luck. He kept discussing her, her beauty, her voice. He doubted many of his own jokes from earlier in the day and asked my second opinion of them. He replayed the complete evening in his mind, over and over again. He was concerned about his image. He kept asking me whether he looked smart and witty or just a funny joker. In spite of my repeated assurances he had his share of doubts. He was definitely in a complete other world. I dozed off while he kept thinking about the evening.

In the morning when I woke up, he was standing by the balcony. It seemed he was awake all night. He was badly smitten in love.

"Mr. Romeo, are you okay?" I asked

"Yeah I am fine. I am happy"

"The way you are behaving the chances that you will push her away is very high"

He turned towards me, "What are you saying? What did I do wrong?" He had concern in his voice

"You are just overdoing it. She may get scared by your actions"

"What am I overdoing?"

"Just be normal. No need to act witty. No need to forcefully impress her. She will come to you"

"Do you think?"

"Yes. It is all about timing. Just be perfect in that"

"How will I know what is the perfect time for anything?"

"I will guide every step for initial few days"

"Thanks man. So what should I do now?"

"Just wait and relax. And in no way call her or message her today"

"But won't she be expecting a call from me"

"No she won't. She is used to guys who are *chipkoos(who cling like a leech)*. Just don't be another one. Take time but take one correct step at a time"

"So what do you suggest?"

"Pick Neha from office a few more times. Ask Neha to time her exit to match with Snigdha's. Try to meet and talk with her and pretend the meetings to be a coincidence."

"But isn't that a manipulation?"

"No it is not. Everything is fair in love."

"But isn't it said that we should be true with the person we are in love with"

"Yes we should be. But before that, we should be true to our feelings of love. We should be true with our life partner. But you are still not her life partner. You are just a candidate, who is trying to win her. And at this stage you have just one goal."

"But didn't you say I am in love. So shouldn't I be behaving as one"

"You have feelings of love. But you are still not in love. You stand somewhere between infatuation and love."

He obviously didn't understand my statement. His question was evident on his face, so I continued "There are four kinds of attraction. They are Love, Lust, Craziness and Infatuation. Infatuation is being attracted towards a person, behaving differently or rather awkwardly in the person's presence. Sometimes it just dies

over, and sometimes it graduates to something bigger. Craziness can be better described as unlimited one sided love which is never reciprocated by the other person. Even possessiveness can be termed as Craziness. And believe me no one likes craziness. Even in a committed relationship, acting crazy can create havoc. Coming to Lust, do you want me to explain this as well?"

"BABA when you are imparting gyaan, explain this as well"

I smiled and continued, "Lust is more of a physical attraction. Once you win the person physically the need and the attraction vanishes. The relationship holds good for physical satisfaction. People who do confuse Lust for Love have a bitter experience in the end."

"Love is the kind of attraction for which you are ready to give away financially and psychologically. What we call *samarpan*. It is the feeling to take care, take responsibility, be a friend and to be there." I continued.

"Hah... So I am in love." He declared

"No you are not." I protested

"Yes I am. I want to take care of her. I want to make her a princess. I want to be her friend. And above all I am *samarpit*." He concluded

"That's good. But there are two issues here"

"And what are those?" He asked in a concerned voice

"First, the feelings should be both way for the relationship to be termed as Love. In your case I still feel it is just one way."

"Should I ask her?"

"NO. That is a very distant question for now" I almost scolded him

He as a good student kept quiet waiting for me to continue. "Secondly you should know the person completely before you can commit yourself to Love. Here in your case you have spoken to her only once. You are still not her best of the friends and still a date looks like a far-fetched dream"

"What are you trying to say?"

"I am saying that love happens to a person and not to a face. And hence I would term your feelings as a kind of infatuation but definitely not Love."

It seemed he understood my point and he said, "Ok, I will try talking to her while I pretend to pick Neha"

-X-

Over the next few weeks, Armaan while picking up Neha from office, met and spoke with Snigdha. Every time he used to come home, he would be lost in his own sweet world of dreams. Many a days he skipped dinners, was awake in the nights thinking about her. He even started missing office on regular basis. He was completely smitten over her. We were getting increasingly concerned by his behavior. We planned to meet at Arpit's home and get his misery channelized to something positive.

At Arpit's home, Armaan was still in his own sweet world. He was listening to our conversations but was not processing the words in his brain.

"Here have some coffee" Neha said.

We picked up our cups but it seemed Armaan was still in his own world. He was so lost in his thoughts that he didn't see the rest of us picking up cups.

"What has happened to this guy. Should we take him to a psychologist?" asked Piyush

"No *yaar,* he is not that bad also. He is madly head over heels for that girl and keeps thinking about her. Accepted fact should be that he is overdoing it, but isn't it that what we are here for" replied Arpit

"Neha, haven't you mentioned the girl is very *hi-fi*" asked Piyush

"You can't say that I have any doubt. I know for sure that she has been in many relationships. Boys keep roaming around her. She has an art of mesmerizing the boys and she handles them pretty well as well", said Neha

"How did he fall for that girl. He was the *Hanuman(Indian Mythology)* of our group. Is *Shikhandi pe kahan atak gaya? (Indian Mythology)*"

"We never know whom we fall in love with" interrupted Shubho "If he likes that girl let him give a try. Who knows both could be ideal for each other?"

The emphasis was clear from Shubho's statement that we should try getting the lover boy meet his love. The next hour we discussed various strategies for him to win her over. Armaan still oblivious of our presence and our discussions was singing some romantic hindi songs. Ruchi while offering us the next batch of coffee mugs, said "Why can't we keep it simple?"

"What do you mean by that?" asked Arpit

"Accepted that the girl is in your terms *hi-fi*, but our Armaan is a simple boy. Why to complex things for him? Since the introduction is done and they know each other pretty well by name and face, why can't he just walk over to her and talk like friends?"

"What you are saying is correct, but can Armaan talk normally to her? Can't you see how he is behaving?" protested Shubho

"He is behaving like this because you all are not allowing him to go and express himself. He may fumble his words in the first instance but then who doesn't?" she replied. Then looking at Shubho she continued, "even you did on our first meeting". Shubho gave a shy smile. Then controlling his emotions he looked at me and Piyush, "*Bhabhie ka order suna nahi(you heard the lady)*, you know what you have to do"

We stood up and wrapped our arms around his shoulders and walked him over to the washroom, filled the basin with water and immersed his head in and out in a practiced manner. It took a few minutes for him to come into his senses and once he did, he pushed us away.

"What?" he shouted

"You were in some other world. We were trying to wake you up to tell you about Snigdha" said Piyush

"Why what happened?"

"Don't you want to take the relationship one more step ahead?"

"Obviously I do"

"Then come to the hall. We have a plan"

He dried himself and came over. A freshly prepared coffee was kept for him. While he sipped the coffee, we tried to talk something funny on a different so that he was relaxed.

When he was done, Akruti said "I have sent you a few witty messages on your phone."

"Ok. I will check them later" replied Armaan

"No no. Do it now."

"Why what is the urgency?" Armaan replied a bit irritated

"You need to choose one and send it to Snigdha. And if she responds, then reply back on your own"

"What is she doesn't?" He asked

"Then send one more from the list"

He instantly liked the idea and was quick enough to select one and forward to her. But still he had doubts in his mind, "But shouldn't I call her?"

"Sure you can, but it will be better to wait a few more days for that"

That was acceptable to him. A few minutes later he received a message in reply to his witty message, and then a series of messages started between him and Snigdha. He looked happy.

Over the next few weeks the messages turned to calls and calls to in person meetings. Things were going good for him. He used to be happy and with the freedom of expressing himself well, his performance in other aspects of life was also improving. Love was doing wonders for him.

Things were going good. But Armaan never shared details of his meetings and interactions with her. He looked happy on surface but deep within he was hollow. He was lonely. He was confused. His eyes always searched for something. Something was wrong and we again were getting concerned. When we enquired more, he revealed the fact that they were like best friends now and met almost every day. But they met mostly in presence of other friends, and even if they were alone she kept getting interrupted by calls and messages from all kinds of people. He always felt that she was physically present with him but mentally she used to be somewhere else.

We were quite convinced that she knew of his liking for her, but she was keeping him at bay. Her actions were confusing. One way she was not letting him come any closer, but on other hand she wanted him to be a part of her life. We were not able to figure out her intentions. May be she wanted more time to know him better. Or maybe she liked getting attention. May be she considered him just a friend. But whatever it was, in all this drama, Armaan was lonely.

Finally we meet

For the next few months after Disha and Avantika fiasco, I kept myself busy with office work and with friends. It was terrifying to think about marriage prospects. My friends knew that I had kept the search of life partner on hold. I had given it to the destiny. A lot of discussions had happened at home, on how arranged marriages had proved worth in the Indian society and how it was still more successful than love marriages. Though I was against the risk of marrying someone just because the girl and her family appealed to my parents, I did have my inhibitions of a love marriage as well, concerned about when attraction phase wades out. I had the right intentions for a married life, but that didn't guarantee the intentions of the girl I would marry. Also I was not comfortable with the uncertainty of the concept of destiny. With my doubts still intact, I had asked my parents to find a good girl for me and I promised to marry anyone they select. People near and close to me knew about my decision and they made sure not to discuss marriage with me.

One day when I was about to start back for home after a bad day in office, my father called up.

"Do you still stand by your decision to marry anyone that we select for you?"

I was in a bad mood and I didn't want to reply. I did take a few moments to think over it, but then I replied, "I know you will select a good girl for me"

"In that case, can you come down home by next month?"

"Why what happened? Have you already selected someone?"

"Yes we have. Her name is Ankana Ganguly. She was your school junior and her family lives in Mahesh bazaar area. "

I tried to remember any Ankana Ganguly I knew from my junior batch but couldn't figure out. "And what does she do? What is her educational qualification?"

"She is a school teacher", came the prompt reply

An image of a boring school teacher with oily hair, big spectacles on her nose, wrapped in a cotton saree crossed my mind. I even reacted the same way "School Teacher!!!"

My father understood my tone, and he did remind me of my assurance "You only said you will have no issues with our choice"

"Yes I did, but aren't school teachers boring?"

"They could be. They may not be. And hence we want you here so that you both can meet and figure it out for yourself"

"Ok let me see when I can come down"

And then we hanged up. I tried to gather myself. Images of my every school teacher crossed my mind. I hated them. It was difficult to convince myself to look ahead for a marriage proposal with those images flashing in my head. And added to the fact that I couldn't remember her even though she was my school junior, meant she wasn't attractive as well. I was seriously contemplating my parent's decision. I needed someone to talk to. So I called up Shubho and went straight to his house.

As I rang the doorbell, the door opened to smiling Shubho and Ruchi. The smile was not normal. It had a certain level of amusement and naughtiness in it. I was already struggling with my emotions of a bad day in office, tiredness and the speculation of my parent's decision. I couldn't figure out what they meant with that smile, so instead I asked them, "What are you smiling about?"

"Aren't you excited?" said Ruchi

"Excited about what?"

"Didn't uncle call you and update you about something"

"Yes he did. But how do you know?" I protested

Their smiling faces looked at each other, "Because we helped them find her"

"Whaaaaaat??" that was one of the longest surprise reaction I ever had. I couldn't believe my ears.

"They asked us to find a good girl for you through matrimonial sites. Even Arpit and Neha were involved in this." Said Ruchi in defense.

"But why? And why I was not aware of this"

"They said that they cannot understand your choices and they do not want to impose someone on you. They believe that we being your friends understand you better, and hence they asked us to help. And since you had left your marriage on destiny and were not interested to talk about it, we never told you"

"And you could find no one better than a school teacher?" sarcasm oozing out of me

"Why what's wrong with them?"

"What's good with them?"

"They are affectionate, they are knowledgeable, and they are patient enough to handle your tantrums"

"But they have oily hair, they wear big spectacles and are always draped in a cotton saree", those childhood images flashing across my mind.

"Have you seen her photo or met her in person?"

"No I haven't. But how different she can be to what I told?"

Ruchi walked in to her study while Shubho kept smiling at me from the couch. She came back with her laptop, and placed it in front of me. There was a beautiful girl's profile photo on the screen. She had long black hairs, brown eyes, and a beautiful smile. Undoubtedly she looked like movie actress. The next photos had her in different poses, in different dresses, and all of them in natural light. They were not edited. There was no doubt in my mind that she was drop dead gorgeous. Her photos confirmed that she was well travelled and was very much aware of the latest trends. I repeated the photos all over again for a second look. Ruchi and Shubho were watching my reactions from a distance. My pupils had dilated and I was engrossed in the photos appreciating the beauty.

"Is she anything like you described?" asked Shubho

"She is infact gorgeous" came my instant reply

"So what you say now?" asked Ruchi

"But still she is a school teacher. Noisy and poky" I tried hard to cover my excitement

"How can you say that if you haven't met her?"

"You all are saying as if you have"

"Atleast we have spoken to her. And believe me her voice is better than her face" said Ruchi with a naughty smile

"Whaaaaaaaaaaat!!!" came out my another surprised reaction

I closed my eyes and took deep breaths to calm myself down. I sat there with my eyes closed for a couple of minutes. When I opened them, I asked a question "So how long has all these been happening. And who all have spoken or met her?"

"It has been happening for roughly six months now. We have spoken to many girls and their parents. We shortlisted a few of them, and then forwarded them to your parents. After their approval and their discussions with all of them, Ankana is their choice"

"Hmmmm!!! Thanks" I said

"What are you thanking for?" asked Shubho in protest

"For two things" I said in a calm voice and continued "Firstly to help my parents. Secondly I know whom to kill for any of my marriage tensions"

They both laughed. I was back into my senses. Her pictures had blown me off and added praise from Ruchi and Shubho, had actually created an excitement within me to look forward to meet her. But then how did I not remember her from school if she was so beautiful. So I asked Shubho, "Dad told me that she was our junior in school. But I don't remember her. Do you?"

"At first even I didn't. But then I revisited old school albums and I did figure her out." He walked over to the laptop, while he continued, "And believe me no one was expected to remember her"

"What do you mean?" I asked

He opened a photo, and pointed his finger to a chubby girl with double ponytail in a clean well pleated oversized dress. It looked like a photo of high school days, and the girl looked anything but attractive. "That's her. This is a photo of our tenth class farewell. She was in Class Eight."

"No way!! I can't believe that this is the same girl. She definitely has grown up to a beautiful lady"

"Even I didn't believe. But that's the truth"

We had dinner and then I left for my home. I couldn't sleep the whole night. The picture of Ankana kept flashing in front of my eyes. The mind was creating dreams in itself. At one point I woke up and looked for her *Facebook* profile. Though the details were hidden, I kept looking at her profile photo. There was an impatience developing within me to meet her. It was four in the morning when I booked tickets for home so that I could meet her. Being the festive season all flights were booked.

The earliest I could get was three weeks later.

In the morning after taking a cold water bath, I called up home and let them know about my plans. My parents were happy to know that I was coming down to meet the girl of their choice. I couldn't tell this to my parents, but after looking at her pictures she had become my choice as well. The first thing I did after reaching office was to apply for a leave. I knew my manager would not approve my leave. But then I was going home come what may. As expected my manager cancelled the request to which I clearly replied, I will be off.

In the next couple of weeks my excitement turned to confusion, then to fear and then back to hopefulness. My mind kept toggling between emotions. I was smitten by the photographs of Ankana. But then I was skeptical of the fact that every girl I had been involved in the past had eluded me in the long journey. I had made high hopes on every of my previous relationships, but all ended badly. I was again making big hopes. I wished her to be my life companion and settle down finally. I was finally ready to take the plunge, not because I was completely smitten, but because I had no more energy and patience for another try. But then I was worried about what if she also eludes me at the end.

I shared my confusions with my friends. They tried to console me in various ways that nothing wrong will happen this time, but I had my own suspicions. Every day I had a new negative thought while they kept trying pumping optimism in me. I was getting worried that I had become a kind of pessimist while trying to settle down for marriage over the last couple of years. Optimism peeped sometimes but mostly was as good as a forgotten friend.

Finally the day arrived. I had come home the previous day. All those days, my mother had been training me on phone about how I should interact with the girl and the girl's family, and also on how the post marriage interactions should be. She wanted me to be a man and not to be a wagging tail behind the girl. She wanted me to be in control of my life, and not forget my parents post marriage. Since the previous evening, she had been preaching the same things again in person. When she used to tell this on phone, I used to pretend listening. Still I used to get irritated. But now I was sitting in front of her, and I had no escape. Luckily my mind had wandered off to different thoughts.

The parents had decided to meet over evening tea in the girl's house. We left home around five in the evening. Dad was dressed in formal attire, but not suited up. He didn't want to appear as eager to get his stupid son married. Maa was dressed in a peach color *benarosi saree*, with little makeup and just necessary jewelry. But I was forced to dress like a person going for a job interview for a CEO post. I had

dressed in a dark blue trouser, white linen shirt with golden cufflink, a steel grey blazer, with a pink pocket square tugged in the chest pocket. Our servant had been instructed to polish my shoe like new, and indeed I could virtually see my face in it. While my parents were giving final touches to their appearance, I walked out and occupied the navigator seat in the car. The driver looked at me and said, "*Sahab, aaj to bada jach rahe hain. Kahan chalna hai?*" (you are dressed impeccably, where do I need to take you?)

I looked at Nathan. He was now an old man. He had been driving my parent's car for around fifteen years. He was like a family. We knew everyone in his family by name and face. Inspite of being a south indian, he had mastered in hindi over these years but still he couldn't understand Bengali.

I said, "*Chacha, mummy hi batayegi kahan jaana hai. Unko aane dijiye*" (let mother come, she will give you directions)

A little while later they came out. My mother looked at me sitting in the navigator seat, and shouted, "*are pagol, baba ke boshte de okhane. Tui aamar kaache bosh. Ektu kotha aachche*" (you idiot, let Baba sit there in the front seat, you come back and sit next to me. I have something to talk about with you). My father looked at me, and his eyes were saying, "I don't want to sit in front. How will it look like the head of the family in front seat next to driver? But he dare not say anything against our mother's wish"

So I replied, "*ae to bangla boje na, tumi kotha bolo, aami saamne I boschi. Naato kapod mude jaabe*"(the driver doesn't understand Bengali. So let me sit at front. Also my dress will crumple if I sit in back seat). I could see a smile of relief in my father's face.

"*O baba. Achcha theek aachche*" (ok), she replied

It took us close to an hour to reach their place. If I would have driven it, we could have reached in not more than half an hour, but then Nathan was an old man and preferred to drive very cautiously. All the way my mother kept repeating her instructions on how I should behave in their house, and I kept wishing their house to come at the earliest. Not because I was eager to meet them, but because I had no more patience to listen over all that again. Finally the car came to a halt. And while coming out, my mother again confirmed, "*Mone aache to shob?*" (Hope you remember everything I have told you)

"Hain maa" (yes mother), I said hiding my irritation.

The house had bougainvillea over the entrance gate, a small well maintained

garden with a variety of flower plants. An old couple came walking towards us. The man shook hands with my father and the lady hugged my mother. A young boy was standing behind looking at all these. The dis-interested look on the boy confirmed him to be the teenager younger brother of Ankana. My mother turned towards me and introduced me to her parents. As told by ma, I didn't bow down to touch their feet and take their blessings. Instead I just folded my palms in a traditional Indian way of *Namaste.* They must have understood that the boy has a high self-respect, as my morther wanted to portray. They walked us inside to the sitting area. It was a nicely decorated room with bits of Bengali culture prominently setting up the mode. Clay made Durga Ma's face was hung above the windows. A sitar sat quietly in the corner, next to an open almirah of books. On the other side was a portrait of Rabindra Nath Tagore. The other side of the room had a Diwan Cot covered with an expensive sheet and cute pillows lining it with the wall behind it. Mothers quietly preferred to sit there. In the center of room in front of the window was an oversized sofa of beige color, but over decorated with pieces of Jaipur style sofa cover. Fathers preferred to take the corner positions of the sofa leaving a big gap in the center. That left with a couple of single sofa decorated similarly. I quietly placed myself in the unit next to my father. My mother signaled me to sit straight and with confidence, and I followed her instructions. The teenage boy kept standing at the entrance watching us all take our place. His father signaled him to the single sofa next to me, "Tukai, why are you standing. Sit down" and then he turned to my father, "He is my youngest son. He has given his tenth exam and is waiting for the results"

"You have an elder son also right? Where is he?", asked my dad to initiate the talks

"He is married and lives in Delhi."

"So in all three children?"

"Yes Ankana is the middle one"

Ankana's mother stepped into the discussion, "she is the one who has kept the house together. She is very caring and mature in handling household issues"

My parents looked impressed, but to me it sounded as if she was advertising for fevicol. I kept my thoughts to myself and tried focusing on the talks elders were having. I kept reminding me to sit straight and show an aura of a man on a mission.

Over the next few minutes parents discussed praising each other's family and how well the kids have been doing in their respective fields. I was getting bored. I looked at Tukai. He also had the same expressions as on my face. I thought of talking to him, but he being quite young I was not quite sure of a common topic. Finally I asked the most obvious question, "So what you plan to take next?"

He looked quietly at me and very shyly replied, "maths and computers"

"So you want to become an engineer?"

"Yes that's what baba says is good for me" he replied. I remembered when my father forced something similar on me post my school results. I ended up becoming an engineer, only to realize that one needs to be smart and not studious to become an engineer. This guy instead looked like a doctor material to me. Anyways I didn't comment back on his career choices.

"*Shuncho, ektu cha hole bhalo hoye?*"(bring some snacks for the guests), said Ankana's father

Ankana's mother went inside with a smile and Tukai followed her quietly. While Ankana's father kept conversation with my father, my mother kept revising me her teachings by expressions of eye and lips. I quietly sat there without any reaction. A few minutes later, Ankana came out with a tray in her hand. She was wearing a red and golden colored silk saree. The sun was setting outside and the rays were directly coming in through the window. In that light, her fair skin was radiating. She looked much better than her photograph. I have to accept I was smitten. My eyes had popped up big and my lips had parted ways. It took me a while to realize that, and when I quickly glanced at my mother, she was having a mixed emotion of anger and happiness. I suppose she was happy that I liked her choice and angry because I was so evidently expressing my consent. I hoped her parents didn't see me, but then Ankana and I were the spot lights for the evening. They must have seen me.

She kept the tray down on the center table, went ahead and took blessings of my father and mother by touching their feet in traditional Indian way. For my parents it may be a symbol of respect and culture, but I was turned on by the thin fair waist exposed while she bent down to take their blessings. I had the urge to hold them and pull her in my arms. I somehow managed to control my thoughts and stopped myself from doing anything stupid. She quietly stepped back and served tea to everyone, while her mother brought snacks and sweets in another tray behind her. She kept her eyes down while offering tea to my parents, but she looked directly into my eyes while offering me the cup of tea. She must have read the chain of thoughts in my head, because she gave me a naughty smile with the side of her lips. My eyes again popped out in shock.

She tried to sit in the single sofa next to me, but then my mother asked her to sit next to her, directly in front of me. My mother held her palm in hers and gave an auditing glance at her face. She looked at her makeup and the jewelry she was wearing. Mothers have a different way of analyzing girls and I really appreciate their way of doing it. But for me as a person, that was very discomforting. I wanted to ask my mother not to find any fault in this girl as I was ready to marry her at that very moment.

After some time when my mother was actually satisfied, she asked Ankana's mother, "can the children talk among themselves. They may be getting bored in front of parents"

"Yes yes. Even I feel so" she continued, "Ankana why don't you take him to the inside room. Tukai go and switch on the lights"

Ankana followed Tukai, and I quietly walked behind them. The house was clean as a mirror. Tukai led us to what looked like Ankana's room. It had a cream wallpaint. There was a wide wooden almirah against the left wall, an open window facing a small garden, with a blue curtain neatly parted by the side, a study table next to it, with an attached vertical book shelf. On the right side was a small double bed, much smaller than my king size single bed. On closer look, it could have been a diwan. There was an empty cloth hanger above the bed. Tukai and Ankana stood by the bed and signaled to take a seat on the bed. Somehow I was not comfortable enough to sit on a bed in a girl's room on my first visit. That would have been possible only in a very casual and friendly environment. But the way my mother had been training me for the day, the way I was dressed, and the way things were happening around me, I was convinced it to be a much formal affair. Instead I smiled and looked at Ankana, "If you don't mind, can I sit on the chair?" I told waving towards the chair kept in front of the study table.

She smiled, "Sure"

She and Tukai sat on the bed. We sat there in silence for next couple of minutes. But obviously she was expecting me to initiate the talks, but I was unable to start as I was feeling nervous. Finally, I thought of starting conversation with Tukai, and lamely asked him, "So what do you plan in future?"

He gave me a puzzled look, "I just told you back in the living room. Did you forget so quickly?"

I looked shyly at him, "No, not like that". Before I could explain further, Ankana stepped in, "Tukai emni kotha bole ki.. Ja to ektu aamader aekla kotha bolar aachche" (You shouldn't talk like this.. Now go and let us talk something important). Tukai left the room immediately with a confused expression on his face.

She turned towards me, "It seems you are quite nervous"

"Sure I am"

"But I was told that you are a confident young man"

I looked straight to her eyes, "But no one told me that you are this beautiful, and I am expected to impress you amidst these vigil eyes"

She burst out in laughter. I have to admit, the glow in her face was radiating as a halo. "Why do you need to impress me?"

"Because your feedback will also be taken by your parents to seal the marriage decision"

"Sure it will be taken, but I didn't know you were looking so eagerly to seal it"

I analyzed the look on her face. It was a mix of sarcasm and shyness. "Well my friends did give a very encouraging recommendation about you. Seems they are highly impressed"

"Aah.. They are very sweet people. But now I feel they are liars"

"And why do you think so?"

"They portrayed a different picture about you. And you are nowhere close to that"

"So is it good or bad?"

"I would say, that you need to work a lot hard now to impress me"

"But the look on your face says that I am doing well"

She shyly looked down towards the floor, her index finger tucked her hairs behind her ears, "But don't you have any questions for me? Don't you want to know me more?"

"Sure I do. But as a person you have your own likes and dislikes which may be different than mine. But then that's not a deciding factor. And I don't expect to know you, understand you in a single day. It will take a lifetime, and I think you are interesting enough subject to be read for a complete lifetime."

She blushed and looked directly into my eyes. Then drew her eyes back to look somewhere on the floor next to my chair. I continued, "Do you have any questions for me?"

"Yes I do have lots of them. Also don't consider me studious enough to read you for lifetime"

"But I was told you are a teacher and have a close association with reading"

"That I am at school, but its different back here at home with family"

"So that means I am family now?"

"Well I didn't say so, but you conclude things quite quick"

"I would accept the compliment", I said with a smile, "but please do ask me what you want to"

"I don't know where to start, but lets start from start. Why don't you introduce yourself"

My eyebrows twitched into a question mark. She sensed my confusion. "We seem to know each other very well because of other people. But if we have to get married, don't you think we should know each other in a different way. In a way that only you know me and the way I know you"

An appreciative smile crossed my lips. A very practical girl indeed. Before I could say something in reply, her mother came with my mother in the room. They sat on either side of Ankana. My mother had lot many questions for her to which she kept answering politely. I was completely lost in my world. I don't remember if I heard anything, but I kept looking at her beautiful face. Couple of times she did gave a slight glance.

Later in the evening on our way back, my mother did mention the positives and negatives she could think of. The positives outnumbered the negative points by a huge margin. My father instead asked me, "You have to live the married life. So it's your opinion which matters most. So what do you think?"

"I kind of liked your choice. I think I can live with her" I preferred to keep my answer short

"Fine then we will go and meet Panditji and see what the stars have to say about this relationship." My parents did believe in astrology.

A series of firsts

A couple of days later I was back in Bengaluru. There was a lot of pending work in office, but I couldn't concentrate. Ankana's face kept flashing in front of my eyes. Man I was smitten. My parents had asked me not to call Ankana till Panditji gave his confirmation.

Next Sunday I visited Shubho and Ruchi's house to thank them. Piyush, Akruti, Arpit, Neha and Armaan had also come over. They all wanted to know how the meeting went. Also Piyush, Akruti and Armaan had not seen Ankana's photo. I had all praises for Shubo, Ruchi, Arpit and Neha to find me such a beautiful girl. Listening to all the praises about Ankana, even Armaan got hopeful of finding someone beautiful. So he handed them the duty to find him his wife also. Armaan had completely given up hope for Snigdha. Once in a while they used to share messages and call, but he had stopped meeting her in person. I personally felt that he should have cut away completely from her, but was happy that he was atleast thinking with his mind.

Just after we had lunch, my father called up, "Panditji has recommended the marriage". As I didn't give any response, he continued, "But the earliest auspicious date is in next December"

"What!!" came my instant response, "That is almost a year later"

"So what. You have stayed alone all these years, you can stay one more year. But the marriage will happen only on the date what Panditji has confirmed"

After he kept the call, I told them about the marriage date. They were also surprised but asked me not to worry. Ruchi assured me that she will do something about it, and I wanted to believe her words.

Later in the evening, I messaged Ankana "Did you hear about the news?"

A few minutes later I got the reply, "My marriage is fixed. Now I don't talk to bachelors"

I immediately replied, "Congratulations on that. But sadly, your's would be husband will still be a bachelor for another year", to which I got a prompt reply "Yeah I heard that. But that's good in a way."

"How come?"

The messages were flowing continuously like a live chat now

"Now I have more time to ask you questions which I couldn't on that day"

"Aha.. So I am yet to be scrutinized"

"uf ho.. the word is Crucified", she tried to sound innocent. But I know for fact she would have burst with laughters

"Can I call you?"

"Buttering may not save you mister"

"I just want to hear you while you are laughing"

"Try harder"

I couldn't stop myself from giving her a call. She cut the call in the first ring itself, and her message followed, "My parents have not approved of the idea of a girl talking to her fiance before marriage"

"But in that case you will never be able to crucify me"

"That I will. But I may not call when I am at home."

"Ok, then update me with your schedules"

And the messaging went on till late in the night before the fact dawned to her that she has to be at school early in the morning. I wanted to talk more and I suppose so did she, but then we had to stop.

-x-

The next few weeks we talked over phone during her lunch hour. Based on our conversations, I got the impression of an intelligent, self-confident yet simple and grounded girl. I felt lucky. She indeed was someone I had dreamt about as my life partner.

Then one day she messaged me, "I was forced to resign from my job today"

I immediately called her but she cut the call. So I messaged, "hey what happened"

"They say that I am not fit to be a teacher"

"Who said that. You are perfect. You are the best."

"No I am not"

"Yes you are. May be its just a bad day. Let me talk to you"

I wanted to talk to her, but she didn't reply to my message for long. By that time I had walked out of my building to the small garden in front of the office. Finally she picked my call. I could hear her laughing loudly at the other end. I kept on saying "Hello" but I could only hear her laugh in response. Finally after couple of minutes she could control her laughter and said, "You took a lot of time to call me in my most agonizing moment"

I was still confused with her laughter. A thought flashed across my head that it may have been a prank. "I am confused" I admitted

"That is again a lame excuse"

"Why did you lie about resignation" I protested

"Who lied about it. I did give my resignation. And I was smartly cajoled to take this step"

"But then why are you laughing madly"

"Because I am happy"

"Uf ho.. You have gone crazy", I was losing my composure

"Wouldn't you ask who cajoled me to take this step?"

"Yeah.. Who did?" I asked with dis-interest.

"Your friend Ruchi"

"What!!! Shubo's Ruchi?"

"Yes yes!! That very lady"

"Wait I will call her and give her a piece of my mind"

"Definitely call her but thank her"

"Thank her for what.. I am not getting you"

"Because duffer, I resigned here so that I can join the school in Bengaluru where Ruchi has got me a job"

It took me a couple of seconds to sink in those words. I was happy to an extent which may not be described. "But why are these things being done behind my back" I protested

"Because I was told you hate surprises", came a prompt reply and she went in another laughter marathon of hers.

"But your parents don't even allow you to talk to me on phone, how they allowed you to come to me"

"Hey mister, I am not coming to you. I am coming to Bengaluru. And my sweet Ruchi didi has got me a job in an international school which pays me five time more, and she has even arranged for my accommodation in her apartment building itself. She also convinced my parents that it will be good for my career and will be an easy transition post marriage. She also assured them that I will be staying in her watchful eyes and just a couple of doors away from her"

"Ruchi will definitely be honored. But before that, let me accept the fact that I am loving the surprises"

"So mister, get ready to be crucified. Here I come."

"When are you coming?"

"On twenty-seventh of this month"

"That's just a couple of weeks away", I responded nervously

"Why is something wrong?" she enquired with concern. Her smile completely gone

"Two weeks is very less to get my house clean, get myself presentable and impress you enough so that I am not crucified"

"Don't worry. I will not judge you on these parameters"

The love for her was oozing enough within me, and I kissed my microphone "Muuaahh"

"What was this?" came a concerned angry voice

"Just a glimpse of my feelings right now"

"Hey mister, no hanky-panky please"

"Get used to these, my princess"

"I am cancelling my plans then", she protested

"You cannot, even if you want to" playfulness quite evident in my voice

"I will get a restraining order against you"

"Then I will come in your dreams to kiss you"

"*Chi.. Chi..,* you are talking like this to a school teacher. What will be the impact on the kids around", and we both burst out in laughter. Her lunch hour had come to an end, and so we had to hang up. I came back to my cubicle, but kept thinking of her. I actually began dreaming about her. We both were sitting across each other. She gave me a kiss on my cheek. My reaction was my fists go up in air as a celebratory gesture followed by a loud yes. Someone patted on my shoulder and that I realized I was dreaming. My fists were still in the air, which I quickly pulled back. All my colleagues were looking at me. I just gave a big smile and said, "I am super happy."

-x-

Finally the day arrived I had been waiting for. It was a Sunday. Shubo and Ruchi came along with me to the airport to receive Ankana. Initially she had planned to come alone, but her parents also decided to come along to help their daughter setup afresh in the new city.

We were standing outside the airport to receive her. I was getting impatient. Every moment seemed longer than ever. Shubho and Ruchi kept making fun of me and my reactions. Finally I could see her by the side of a trolley pushed by her father. She was wearing a pink top and a blue jeans, simple but elegant. Shubho quietly reminded me, "Do not let your emotions out in front of her parents". I smiled back at him. I knew this was a day when her parents had to be won. As they came near, in a lame attempt to impress them, and ignoring my mother's instructions, I bowed down slightly to touch their feet for blessings. Her mother stepped back, "o maa, jamai ei shob kore na ki?" (it doesn't look good for the son-in-law to do this)

I responded just with a gentle smile. I glanced at Ankana. Even though she was talking to Ruchi, her eyes were on me. This was the first time Shubho and Ruchi were meeting Ankana in person. We walked down to the hired Innova taxi in the parking. Me and Shubho preferred to walk back with the luggage and let Ruchi lead them. Shubho elbowed me. He had a big grin on his face. I asked "what?"

He replied, "Man you have hit a jackpot"

"She is your sister in law. Mark your words and give some respect", I replied with a naughty smile on my face

He slapped the back of my head.

The rest of the journey back, Ruchi was the center-stage. They all were conversing as if they knew each other for a lifetime and meeting after a long time. It didn't sound at all that they were formally meeting for the first time. Me and Shubho sitting at the back seat just watched them bond. Finally Shubho's apartment building arrived.

They liked the apartment Ruchi had chosen for Ankana. Later we had snacks over tea at Shubho's apartment during which I received a message on phone. It was from Ruchi who was sitting right across me in the room, "Now find your way out. Your presence may not be appreciated by her parents for this long. And while they are in town make your visits discreet"

I looked at Ruchi across the room. Her expressions were stern and which had *Believe Me* written all over it. I had trust on Ruchi's instincts and so I took leave.

Later in the evening, Ankana messaged me with the new number Ruchi had arranged for her. "Its me. Why did you leave early today?"

I did want to write that her parents wouldn't have liked my company around you, but I preferred "With a beautiful girl like you sitting in the room, there is always a fear of losing self-control"

"Are you always this corny?" came her reply

"I just mentioned the truth"

"Ok. I am tired and need to sleep now. Wish me luck for my first day in the new job tomorrow"

"All the best. And good night. Sweet dreams"

For the next week we spoke for a couple of minutes in her school's lunch break time and a few messages before sleeping every day. I didn't want to get into bad books of my future in-laws. Instead I kept myself patient. Finally the day came I had been waiting for a week. My patience over the last few days had taught me to appreciate the common jokes on in-laws. I was happy that they were leaving.

On Sunday, I accompanied Shubho, Ruchi and Ankana to the airport to see off Ankana's parents. Before entering the airport, Ankana's mother held Ruchi's hands. "You have already done so much for her like her elder sister. But I have one more request. She is my only daughter and I am leaving her in a big city this far from her house, only on your belief. Please take good care of my daughter."

"*Are kakima,* just be assured. Ankana is a smart girl, and I will take care of her. You need not worry" she assured with a pat on back of her hand.

While they went in for check-in, we went for CCD coffee. Ankana wanted to be in airport till her parent's flight took off. We sat around a small table. Shubho sat on my right, and Ankana on my left. I was feeling free once her parents had entered the airport, and we were not under their watchful eyes. Even Ankana looked relaxed but emotional.

Suddenly Ruchi's words broke the silence, "Mr. Bachelor, you need to take permission from me even for what you are doing now". Un-consciously I had been ogling. She continued, "She is my responsibility here, so better watch your actions"

Sheepishly I retracted my eyes away from Ankana and on Shubho, "it seems you need to work hard to keep your lady's attention off me"

Ruchi stood up from her chair and punched me on my left shoulder, "don't ever talk to my cutu like that"

Instead I pinched Shubho's cheek mocking her "Cutu"

Ankana was quietly sitting watching us all with a smile on her face. When I looked at her, her smile vanished for a moment and then it was taken over by a naughty glow in her eyes. She turned towards Ruchi, "He is mine and keep your punches off him"

No one was expecting such a reaction from her, and Ruchi was taken aback for a moment. I couldn't stop my smile, and Shubho instead pinched Ruchi's cheek. I raised my left palm asking for a high five, "Now this is a team".

Ankana's father called informing us about their boarding call. After wishing best of journey, we drove back to Shubho's house. The rest of the evening we played cards. Ruchi and Shubho played as a team, Ankana and me as another. It was fun, and I got to know her even better. After dinner, Ankana expressed her wish to call it a day. We realized it was quite late in the night, and so even I left for my home.

Next day I took leave from office for second half and with intent to surprise her, went to pick Ankana from school. She came out with a couple of colleagues while children ran across to their respective modes of transportation back home. I quietly stood by my bike on the other side of the road. I wanted to see the look in her eyes when she sees me. She stopped for a moment near the school main gate right across to where I was standing, to wave off a colleague to a school bus. She started walking down the lane where other buses were parked. Her eyes though were searching something along her path. She boarded the third bus and sat next to a window and her colleague beside her. For that fraction of second, she looked out of window and straight to my direction. But then she looked off. It took her a second to realize that she had looked directly at me, and so she looked back in my direction. This time I waived to which she too waved back. A smile came across her face and I could clearly see that from that distance. She is beautiful but when she smiles she looks like an angel. She turned left to her colleague while her hands tucked her hair behind her ear. Her colleague also looked at me with a smile, and the next moment Ankana had de-boarded the bus and was walking towards me.

"What are you doing here?"

"Didn't you like me here?" I asked

"I never said that" she shyly looked down

"I wanted to make sure your day was fine"

"That it was"

"But let me promise, the day has just begun"

"What do you have in mind?"

"Let us first get you out from here. Your colleagues and the kids are watching from their respective bus"

She glanced a quick look and many eyes were on us. So she quickly hopped on the pillion and we drove off.

I drove her to Lalbag. It is a big park in the middle of city and a relief of green pasture. I parked my bike in the parking and we started walking.

This was the first time we were meeting alone in person. Even though it was obvious we liked each other and looking forward to a happy married life, there was a visible hesitation. We didn't know where to start, what to talk. We shared many awkward glances by the side of the eyes before she broke the silence

"So how come you were so early at my school. Don't you have work?"

"I do. But some things are at a higher priority and for that leaves can be taken."

"You took a leave. What reason you gave?"

"Personal things don't require a reason"

"Oh so you are the hero type. No questions asked. Is it?"

I blushed slightly but nodded in NO. "I just couldn't resist the idea of meeting you"

She smiled and looked away. Next few minutes we walked in silence till we sat on a bench by the lake. There was a good feet gap between us. The awkwardness and the hesitation was evident.

"So how was the day at school?" I asked

"It was good. Still catching up. Met some more teachers and the School In-charge still helping me with the Induction process"

"Liked the atmosphere there?"

"So far so good. Good thing is most of the teachers are around my age, so its easy to gel'

"That's good"

Another few moments of silence followed. A whole bunch of discussions and ideas were going across my head, but nothing was filtering out through my lips. I did realize that and took a long deep breath. I pulled my fingers into a fist to gather some confidence

"I think this is awkward. But I don't think it should be"

It seemed like I had suddenly unlocked a whole new door. Even she was nervous and my statement accepting the awkwardness got her the confidence that she was not alone. We did have something in common and lot of stuff to talk about. We didn't realize how hours passed by. We were sitting closer to each other and I had positioned myself perpendicular to her and was facing her profile. We both were now at ease and having a good time together.

I quietly put forward my right hand towards her with my palms facing up. I could see the inhibition, awkwardness and hesitation back on her face. I sat there with a dry smile on my lips and hands kept out still in air, while she kept looking down. For a very small instant she looked straight at me.

"What?" I said

She didn't respond. So I continued, "It seems we have a life to walk together and I wish I can do that holding your hands in mine"

The next moment she had tears in her eyes. I quickly got up and sat on my knees in front of her. I couldn't understand why she was crying. I tried to wipe off her tears, but she didn't allow me to. An old couple was on their evening walk and they stopped seeing her cry. But soon with the decades of experience, they realized that it was one of the awkward moments in a young relationship, and walked away with a smile on their face. It took a few minutes before Ankana could control her emotions. Wiping her tears off, she spoke in a voice filled with emotions and tears, "It may be easy for you, but this is my first relationship and I am not used to this"

"Used to what?" I asked surprised

"To try to be romantic and cool with your moves"

"And why do you think it is easy for me? And why do you think I am trying to be romantic?"

"Because I know you have had lot many relationships in past"

I didn't expect that. I didn't know what to reply and how to reply. I just pulled myself up and walked towards the lake. I stood there looking at the water. It felt like someone had punched my stomach. Minutes passed by, before I realized it was getting dark. So I turned towards her. She was sitting quietly, a little scared but still beautiful.

"Come lets go. I will drop you home"

She signaled me to sit by her side. I nodded in negative. "Just for a minute. Please!!!" She put a lot of emphasis on Please. So I obliged.

"I am sorry. I shouldn't have said that. But this is my first relationship and things are moving pretty fast. I am scared"

I looked into her eye, took a pause and said, "I understand that. And hence was giving my hand for your assurance"

"I am sorry" and tears rolled back from her eyes

Instead of wiping off the tears I continued, "I may have a past, but this is a first for me too, when I am trying to win a girl with whom I know I will be spending my life and I want her to be life."

She started crying heavily, then started punching my chest and shoulders and then before I could realize she hugged me tight. We sat there for a few more minutes. I could see the guards coming around asking people to leave so that they can close the park for night. Hence we left.

I had planned a romantic dinner as well, but since emotions were high I decided against it. I dropped her at her building and drove off after a very formal bye. I stopped a few hundred meters away and gave Ruchi a call

"My princess has had an emotional day. Can you make her feel home?"

"Sure I can. But soon you have to stop depending on me and man up to can take care of her" she protested

"You know I will soon"

She smiled and kept the call. I knew she would take good care of my girl.

-x-

Later in the night I received a message, "Awake?"

I was watching TV but was thinking of her. I replied "Nope"

Immediately she called me, "I am sorry sweetu"

I just got a name. I had already had a lot of firsts in the day, and now the new name was a cherry on top,"Sweetu!!!"

I preferred to keep the emotional past of the day behind, and concentrate on the events in the present, "But another name would have been good"

"Why what is wrong with this name?"

"I had instead planned to give this name to you"

She smiled, "Are you always this cheesy?"

I preferred not to respond. So she continued, "I have to accept you are romantic"

"Thank you"

"Or it could be, everyone else is as well, but I am new to this world of romance". Either she was extremely innocent and sweet or else she was making sure to offend me every single moment. I wanted to believe the first and so I tried to ignore her directed puns.

"In that case, I will try to be less romantic"

"No no. I like it the way it is"

"So you had dinner?", I tried to change the topic

"Yes. After you dropped me home Ruchi Di came over. Then we had girly talks and then a sumptuous dinner. I just came back from their home"

"That's good"

"What you had for dinner?"

And then we spoke on daily routine stuff, work, habits and other stuffs till late in the night. We were back on the territory where we could talk freely and hesitation was not a visible concern.

The love grows

The rest of the week was tough in office. I deliberately didn't try to prioritize meeting Ankana in person. She was scared that things were going fast for her and I appreciated her space. We did speak over phone every night before sleep.

Come Saturday, she invited me to her home. The plan was a small get together and a thank you lunch treat to Ruchi and Shubho for what they have done for her. It had been just a week that she had started living completely on her own, and away from her parents. Everyone was a stranger around her but she was driven by the promise of a nice future. Even though she didn't let anyone know, but it must have been difficult on her. Even I wanted to thank Ruchi and Shubho for what they did for us. So I reached early around ten in the morning, to help her in the kitchen.

She was surprised to see me so early. She wasn't expecting me till noon. She was in a t shirt and shorts. She looked cute and sexy. She asked me to make myself comfortable and she rushed inside to get changed. By the time she came back in a formal salwar-kurta, I had made my way into the kitchen. What was surprising was that in those couple of minutes, she had managed to change her cloths, groom her hair and try a slight makeup. She was faster than an express train. I just couldn't stop myself from smiling.

"What are you doing in kitchen? And why are you smiling?" she was panting.

"Relax. I have come early to help you out in the kitchen."

"No no. You sit. You are a guest, and behave as a guest"

"But this thankyou treat is from us, so I am not a guest"

"No this is from me"

"What they have done is not limited to your happiness. I am happier than anyone for what they have done."

"That's good, but still I don't like you doing work"

"Believe me I am not that bad in kitchen"

She smiled, and pointed her finger towards living room, asking me to leave kitchen. I smiled back and signaled that I will be in kitchen. She gave up, "Ok, be around. But I am getting late, so let me resume my work"

"So what should I do?"

"Can you cut onions?"

"Sure I can" a knife was in my hand and I was looking for a chopping board.

"Do you have a spare shirt. Your shirt looks expensive, and that may get dirty and oily" she pointed out

"I haven't brought a spare shirt. But if you have a spare towel or shawl, I can wrap around"

She quickly brought me a shawl and wrapped it around me. Next couple of hour or so we worked as a team and she was very clear in her instructions. I just followed them. The vegetables were ready, and so was the dal, side dishes and chapatti. She put up pulao in a pressure cooker, and rushed inside for a quick bath and to get ready. Chicken was slowly cooking in the other burner. She instructed me to put off the Pulao after two whistles and keep an eye on the Chicken.

By the time she came out, I had cut the salads, made raita of the curd. Pulao and Chicken were ready. And I had cleaned up the dining table and washed the utensils that were not required. On seeing this, initially she got angry but then she gave a friendly slap on my shoulders and gave me a big smile "thank you". She didn't know, I would have done the complete cooking for a glimpse of that beautiful smile. I couldn't control myself and I pinched her cheek. There was a big grin across my face.

I unwrapped myself from the shawl and excused myself to the restroom to freshen up before the official guests arrived. When I came back she had already shifted the food to the dining table and was placing plates. The kitchen looked clean as if it was never used.

Shubho and Ruchi arrived a while later, while we were watching TV. Ruchi was impressed that the cooking was done. She pulled me to balcony, "It seems you both are gelling together and working efficiently as a team"

"Means?" I acted innocent

"I know you helped in the kitchen"

"No I didn't. She did everything on her own. I just arrived a few minutes back"

"Oh is it, then what is your wrist watch doing on the Kitchen shelf? Don't tell me you were doing kinky stuff in the kitchen"

I slightly tapped on back of her head, "don't make stories"

She pulled my ears instead, "Remember your marriage is months away, so act slowly"

I didn't respond to that. I just pulled her back to the dining table. Shubho was already busy munching the side dishes. I quietly picked my watch from the kitchen shelf and sat next to Shubho.

The lunch was sumptuous and tasty. An old saying goes by, "The path to a man's heart goes through the stomach" and she proved the point perfectly. Ankana indeed was a complete woman and I was completely impressed. God had heard my wish.

Post lunch we watched a movie on television. It was followed by a round of tea and snacks. Shubho and Ruchi had to leave as they had other plans for the evening. Once alone we felt the awkwardness back. It was obvious that we had yet not reached that stage of comfort in our relationship. We still had a few inhibitions.

To get out of the situation I suggested we go for a walk. And so we did. It was a quiet walk and a cool breeze was flowing by. She was looking beautiful in the halogen lights and her hair kept waving with the wind. We were near the park, when she got a call from her mother. She stepped aside to attend the call, as she didn't want her mother to know that we both were spending time together alone. With nothing else to do I got busy playing with a couple of four year old kids. We were jumping around and giggling. I didn't realize when she was done with her call. She stood at a distance watching me. But when I saw her waiting, I bid goodbye to the kids and joined her.

A few yards later, she wrapped her right hand around my left upper arm and took my left palm into her. I stopped for a while staring down at her with a question in my eyes. She looked up at me, smiled "You are good" and then we resumed our walk in silence.

In the good weather with each other's company, we didn't realize that we had walked kilo-meters and were very far away from her home. We were hungry and tired. The only eating joint visible was a small dhaba style eatery. It didn't look hygienic, but then we were out of options and we were hungry. I asked her if it was

okay for her. She didn't complain. That was something I had not seen in my previous relationships. Others would have made faces or explicitly mentioned against the idea. This girl was simple and grounded.

The food was not good, and we couldn't eat much, but it was bliss to have something in stomach. She never complained a bit about the taste of the food or hygiene of that place. She was as human and grounded as I considered myself. I was falling for her. Since it was late and we were tired, we took an auto-rickshaw back to her home. In the auto-rickshaw she did not hesitate to keep her hands on mine. Her warm hands were signifying the warmth of a true relationship. I didn't realize when I locked her fingers into mine, pulled our hand up to my lips and planted a kiss on back of her palm. That was the first kiss of our relationship, and she was not prepared for it. Her hand shivered and she pulled her hand back. I could hear her breathing intensify and it took her a couple of minutes to calm down and again place her hands on mine. We sat motionless after that till we reached her home. After dropping her home and a quick good bye to Shubho and Ruchi I drove back home. A while later after I reached home, Ankana called me to make sure I had reached home safely. It was definitely a start of a relationship, a journey of emotions and true feelings.

She was happy how the day turned out. She mentioned that she got to know me better and she enjoyed my company. I could sense she was opening up to me. She was developing trust on me. And with the excitement of knowing these facts, it also brought in a responsibility and expectation to which I had to live up to. She shared with me a lot of details of her childhood and we spoke till early morning. Finally it was time to hang up. All night I wanted to tell her how much I was in love with her, but couldn't. But when we hanged up, it felt as if I didn't mention the most important thing which she should know. So I messaged, "I love you"

I had to wait a couple of minutes before the reply came, "As if I didn't know ;-P"

I knew I had still a long way to go to win her love, but her response made sure I slept peacefully. She was slowly but steadily becoming my life.

I was still in my beautiful dreams when my phone rang loudly. Without even opening my eyes, I picked up the phone

"Still sleeping, Idiot? Get up. We need to be at Arpit's home by noon", it was Armaan on the other side

"Why what happened?" I asked

"You forgot? Today is his birthday and we had planned a surprise for him"

"Oh shit. It's today?" We had made this plan a couple of months back on Piyush's birthday. Arpit had acted smart in that party and he deserved something extreme in return. It had to be a revenge surprise. I quickly glanced at my watch. It was already twenty minutes past ten.

"thanks man for waking me up. Are others on time?" I enquired

"Still need to call them. But be near his house around noon. We will attack together"

"Done. I will be there"

"And bring Ankana too"

I realized that I had never mentioned about this party to Ankana, "Oh shit. Let me call her. Bye bye"

I immediately called up Ankana. She was already awake and was enjoying her tea over the morning paper

"Hey I am sorry" I replied to her Hello

"Why what happened"

"I forgot to mention earlier, but today is Arpit's birthday. And we had planned a surprise party at his home."

"You need me to come?" she questioned

"But of course. And you need to be ready in another half an hour"

"What!! Why?"

"I am sorry dear. But we plan to meet at noon at his house"

"And you are mentioning this now at the last moment?" She was ridiculed

"I had forgotten about this. Armaan just woke me up reminding about this party. You can kill me later for this, but for now get ready quickly. I will get ready in ten minutes and come pick you up"

I could hear her taking a deep breath. "No need to be a superman. Anyways I will take a bit more time to get ready. Just do one thing"

"Tell me"

"Call Shubho and ask if I can come along with them. In such a scenario, we all can get ready properly and in a relaxed way. And you come directly to Arpit's house"

I paused for a moment. That was a valid idea "You are intelligent"

"And you are stupid. A big one indeed", she chuckled

"My pleasure"

I immediately called Shubho. Armaan had just called them as well. Even they had forgotten about the party. He assured me that they will bring her along, and they plan to start in an hours' time. I messaged the same to Ankana and went ahead to freshen myself.

At five minutes past noon, we all met near Arpit's home. Armaan had a big cake in his hand. Piyush had big polythene in his. It was full of water balloons. On touching it I realized it was filled with cold water, and I was assured it was dirty too. Akruti had a polythene full of some Holi color packets, a bottle of pickle, a milk packet, few eggs and a packet of mud and another of wheat flour. Ruchi and Ankana were aghast to see the planning, but Shubho and me were prepared for the show.

When Arpit opened the door, Shubho, Ruchi , Ankana and me were standing in the front, and Armaan, Piyush and Akruti with all the stuffs hiding behind. Arpit claimed that he was expecting us to throw some surprise. He said that Neha was telling him that since no one wished birthday the previous night, something major was coming. While Armaan placed the cake on the dining table, Piyush and Akruti quietly slid the polythenes behind the sofa. Arpit was so excited to see the cake that he didn't think otherwise.

Ruchi pulled Neha to a side and warned her that something nasty is planned, so better be prepared for a dirty house when we leave. We had not expected, but Neha came along as a sport. She went back to Arpit, and said "I know they will put cake on your face. So why don't you change to some other clothes"

Arpit quickly went inside to change. Neha instead led me and Piyush to another restroom. She was clear that house should not get dirty, but it was Ok to do whatever was planned in the restroom.

We filled up the bath tub with water and added holi color packets to it. In another bucket we mixed the remaining contents into a semi solid paste. We quietly came back and stood by the side of table where Arpit was planning to cut the cake. We waited for him to enjoy a slice, and offer one slice to each one of us. Since we were acting so normal, for a few minutes he must have thought that nothing bad is going to happen. But then with a swift action, the whole cake was on his face and hairs. He was blinded by big chunks of cream over his eyes. On the pretext to clean him up, Neha led him to the same restroom where we had planned to get him dirty. While he bent over the basin to clean himself, we bombarded him with the cold water balloons. The balloons were filled with brownish white water. Piyush had mixed mud, talcum powder and wheat into cold water before filling up the balloons. Armaan swiftly picked up the bucket and started rubbing the semi-solid paste all over Arpit's body. Neha was capturing all this on her camera. In all this time, Arpit could just manage to clean his eyes. He could see us all attacking him with all the stuff. In a glance he saw the bath tub filled with colored water and he tried to push his way out of the restroom. He knew us very well and if we had brought in such colors it had to be kind of sticky and won't get off easily. But we got hold of his limbs and put him in the bath tub. He tried to struggle his way out, and quite a bit of colored water spilled on our cloths as well but we didn't mind that. He kept shouting, "Its my birthday. Show some respect"

Finally when we were satisfied, we left him alone in the restroom and came back to the sitting area. It took him couple of hours to clean himself. But still he had a shade of green, brown and silver all over his body.

Ankana sat quietly in a corner with disbelief on her face. When I asked her about the look on her face, she said, "Is this the way you all celebrate birthday?"

To which Piyush replied, "This is the way we celebrate his birthday. For us we celebrate it in a much civilized way"

"But why was he treated like this?"

"He deserved it"

Arpit jumped in with protest, "Why did I deserve?"

Piyush replied, "Try remembering my birthday"

Arpit's expressions told he was trying to remember. It took him a while and then he looked down with a dry smile on his face and declared, "Yes I deserved it". No one wanted to share the exact details with the female counterparts in the room.

For lunch we had ordered pizzas and they had arrived, so we gorged on it. Ankana walked by me, and pinched my upper arm. She slowly spoke into my ears, "You are an animal"

To which I promptly replied, "isn't that good"

She slapped my back and went to wash her hands. By the end of the day, I could see she had made good friends with Akruti and Neha as well.

The next week went as a routine. Every evening I used to come down to meet Ankana. We would roam about, eat out in restaurants and after I dropped her back, we used to talk over phone till late in the night. We had planned to go for a movie on Saturday, but some urgent work came up in my office on Friday and I had to work from office on Saturday as well. By the time work was over it was well past midnight. I called up Ankana as soon as I reached home. She had been waiting for my call all day and was quite angry. But since I was mentally drained of energy as well as physically, instead of trying to compose her I preferred hearing her. I didn't realize when I dozed off into sleep while still on the call.

I woke up to a series of doorbells. I tried to ignore them, but they didn't stop. Irritated I opened the door with my eyes still unwilling to open because of sleep. Ankana was standing there wearing a beautiful blue dress and the bright sunrays falling on her golden skin. The reflected light from her dangling earrings blinded me initially, but realized that it was not a dream and she actually was standing on my doorstep. I panicked and closed the door on her face. I soon realized I was only in a boxer. In a hurry I wrapped a towel on my upper body and opened the door.

"I am sorry, but come in and please keep your eyes closed"

She came in, but eyes wide open. I repeated, "Close your eyes na"

"Why?"

"I am not wearing anything"

She smiled, looked other way and said, "You don't look bad without your shirt, but go quickly get dressed. A beautiful girl has come to your house, make yourself presentable"

I blushed but rushed inside. I quickly brushed my teeth, wet my hair, combed it, pulled up a pair of jeans and wore a t-shirt. She was standing near the book shelf and looking at my collection of books. She saw me coming, "some nice books"

"Thanks. Will you like tea or water"

She turned to face me, her eyes aghast, "stop being formal. And don't act like a weirdo"

"But how did you know my address? And why a surprise visit? I could have cleaned up my house"

"You need to know details of your fiancé, and address is a simple thing"

"No tell me, how did you know the exact door number?"

"Shubho dropped me here"

"And where is he?"

"He is a smart person. He didn't want to be a part of our situation"

"But why a surprise visit?"

"You avoided me yesterday, and I wanted to spend a quality time. So here I am"

I couldn't reply anything. She went into the kitchen, stood there with big eyes, then to balcony. She quickly came back and then she started walking towards bedroom. I rushed to block her way, "don't go inside"

"why? Are you hiding your girlfriend inside?"

My eyebrows twitched, and my hands came by side of my hips, in a confronting posture. She pinched my cheeks, and pushed me aside. My bedroom was a mess. Shirts and jeans were thrown everywhere. Bedsheet was all crumbled. Powder pack, deodorant and other cosmetic items were on the ground. My dirty unwashed undergarments were thrown in a corner. I quickly pulled a shirt out of bed and placed it above my undergarments. She further walked in my bathroom, had a quick glance and she was out. I was standing at the door of my bedroom. She looked at me, "Not bad. But lot of improvement required". I was surprised by her comment. She continued, "when I formally come to this house, these all has to be taken care. And I am not cleaning this stuff up"

I just replied in "okay"

We walked outside to the living room. She continued, "Arent you hungry?"

"Yes I am"

"So whats in breakfast?"

"There is a good dosa center nearby. Lets go there"

"No no. Lets eat something at home. In peace"

"But I don't think I have anything in stock"

"Hmmm" she thought for a while. Then walked into the kitchen. "Would you like butter toast, *poha* or *upma*"

"*Poha*" I said

"And tea or coffee?"

"Tea"

"Do you have sugar and tealeaf?"

I checked quickly. I had little of it in stock.

"Go quickly get beaten rice, milk and onion from a grocery store"

When I came back in around fifteen minutes, kitchen looked like new, my bed had a clean bed-sheet; my used cloths were stacked up in a corner neatly. My cosmetics were put up in a corner in the table. The living room looked neat and things at their respective place. The house looked good and somewhat similar to when my mother visits me. A woman surely knows how to make a house, a home. I stood with my eyes wide open and surprised. "You said you won't be cleaning my house. Then what's this?"

She didn't reply. She just smiled, took the contents from my hand and went inside the kitchen. Next minutes while she worked as a well-oiled machine doing multitasking, I stood at the kitchen door appreciating her work. She was clean, efficient, systematic, perfect and above all beautiful. *Poha* was tasty and the tea was energizing. I was happy to have her in my life but a small part within me was nervous. She was a perfectionist, best in whatever she did. She was smart, beautiful, grounded, homely and cute. And I was not everything like that. Also I was already in love and decided to grow old with her.

After breakfast, we talked long about me and my past. Though I didn't lie about the dark patches in my past, but I was very cautious to choose my words. But soon it felt like I was being interviewed, so I tried to change the topic. I suggested some fun games on X-box Kinect. She liked the idea and we played a few games of badminton, then a series of karaoke songs and then dance steps in dance central game. It was fun. She had a nice voice, some great flexible dance moves, and that made me a bit more nervous. In all my past relationships I had a feeling that I am much better than my girlfriends, and here was the girl who was miles ahead of me. She was a princess, and I was a common man. I must have had done some great deeds to have her in my life.

At the end of the marathon gaming session, we were tired and thirsty. She offered to make tea, while I placed myself in front of the television and started browsing the channels. In one of our late night phone conversations she had told that,

"*Socha na tha*" was one of her favorite movies. I found a channel playing it, so I switched to that channel. When she came out of kitchen, she was happy to see the movie. I was sitting in my lazy boy sofa, and she came and sat on my lap. She handed me my cup of tea, and focused herself on the movie sipping tea from her cup. Her sitting over me was unexpected, and I was taken by surprise. My focus shifted away from movie and was on her. It was the first time she was so close to me that I could smell her. Her hair smelled beautiful. Her skin had a fresh smell. Her golden skin looked smoother than a marble. There was no sign of sweat even after playing for so long. Her face profile had sharp features, an expressive eye, long razor sharp prominent nose, pink and soft lips, an upper cheek bone and the pink spot over it was the only other shade visible on her golden skin. Strands of hair were falling on her face, and I softly tucked it behind her ears. My breathing had picked up. My emotions had accelerated but were not able to find a way. I couldn't hold myself longer, and softly spoke into her ears, "should I tell you one thing?"

She nodded affirmative but didn't turn her face towards me. She was still focused into the movie. I continued, "You are the most beautiful person I have ever come across, and I am in love with you. I love you *Shonu* "

She turned her face towards me, her body shifted over me and she was sitting straight in front of me, her eyes looking deep into mine. Her pupils dilated. My heartbeat and breathing had picked up and so did hers. I collected myself and continued, "I haven't formally proposed my love to you earlier, but would like to ask you whether you would like to grow old with me, sitting like this on my lap and looking as beautiful as you are". I could see a glimpse of tears covering her pupils, and we didn't realize when we kissed each other. The initial soft kiss soon turned out to be intense and the emotions ran high. It took us a while to come back to senses. And when we did, she wrapped me up in her arms, and rested her head on my shoulders. My arms wrapped her in a tight grip. She was breathing heavily. We quietly sat there for long. We sat there feeling each other's breath and pulses. We had lost track of time.

But then the sense of hunger did surpass the romantic emotions, and we decided to go out for a very late lunch. The rest of the day we roamed around, did window shopping and spent some quality time together. The whole time though we couldn't keep our hands away from each other, and since we didn't trust us with emotions, we deliberately kept away from home. Later in the night after a romantic dinner I dropped her home. I knew if I entered her home, I could not stop myself spending the whole night there. But I was not quite ready to test our relationship yet. I didn't want the day to end, but it had to. The expression on her face clearly begged me to

stay but she also was not sure if she was prepared for that. With a heavy heart I kissed her good bye and off I went. After such a wonderful day, I still wanted to be in her touch. I couldn't stop myself from giving her a call while riding back home. All the way back, while I parked my bike, while I changed myself, while I lay in bed, we kept on talking. It seemed like we were teenagers again.

The whole next week, we shared messages at every possible instance, we spoke on phone for hours, we went on long walks in the evenings and made sure we had dinner together. We were the new love birds in town.

In one of our late night phone calls that week, she expressed her desire to visit Mysore palace. She had always seen pictures of the majestic palace, but since she was so near to it, she wanted to pay a visit. The next Saturday I borrowed Shubho's car and took Ankana on a day trip to Mysore. We went straight to the palace in the morning and spent some quality time there. We clicked photos of the palace from every angle and either or both of us in every possible pose. Next I took her to Chamundi hills, and then to zoo and St. Philomena's church. We did enjoy the day. In the evening we planned to witness the water and light show of Brindavan gardens. We reached there early, so we roamed around in the beautiful garden and waited for the dusk. We had planned to witness the first of the series of water light shows and then leave back for Bengaluru.

The water show was good and on time. When we returned to our car after the show, I found that people had parked all around my car and unless they move out, I could not drive out. I had parked near the right edge of the parking lot, next to the water body. Because of that the area was full of mosquitoes and other small insects, making it difficult to stand out in open. We had to take shelter in car. We decided to sit in the back seat and wait for other drivers to come and take out their car.

We had nothing else to do so we started discussing the events of the day. We were making fun of each other and the funny experiences we had in the day earlier. In one such topic, she was making fun of my interaction with a monkey during our zoo visit. I was doing some actions which the monkey was imitating. She instead was making fun about me imitating the monkey. She was in a mood of pun and was not missing any opportunity on me. Since I had nothing more to make fun of her and had run out of my wits, to keep her quiet I had to pull by her arm. Before I realized she was above me, and our faces in front of each other, so close that we could feel the air we were breathing. Our breathing intensified and we came closer and closer very slowly. Our lips touched and we shared a passionate kiss. I tightly wrapped her in my arms. I wanted her to stay right there. But she was kissing all over my

face. I couldn't hold myself back and responded by kissing her all over her face, her neck and down. Even she responded my passion and soon we realized we were all over each other. Before we could react or understand our sudden outburst of emotions, we were making love. We were one and we were in love.

A nearby parked SUV came to live and that broke the silence of the parking lot. We came to our senses. I was happy to have loved her so intensely and passionately. There was a glimpse of shyness mixed with a smile of being loved. She dressed herself back, and groomed her hair very sheepishly. I sat there watching her. We were sweating, but that didn't matter. It was the feeling of being madly in love, of blessings from god. We sat there for few more minutes in silence, me with a smile on my face and she with shyness in her eyes. I took both her hands in mine and planted a kiss on back of her palm, looked straight into her eyes and said, "I love you". Her lips sparkled with a glimpse of smile, and then she replied in a voiceless movement of lips "I love you too". The car in front made a move ahead clearing my path. So I hopped into the front seat and pulled the car from parking. I stopped just outside on the road, and let her come in front and made her comfortable. We drove in silence for some time, before we stuck briefly in a traffic crawl. I forwarded my palm, on which she kept her hands. I held it tightly. She looked at me, "What" I looked at her, didn't reply but just smiled. We were having an awkward moment. We didn't know what to talk. The traffic eased out, and I tried to pull my arms so that I can engage a higher gear, but she didn't leave my hand. She was holding it tight now. I changed gears while she still held my hand, and then when I reached the highest gear, I let her play with my hand, and I drove cautiously with one hand on steering wheel. Her grip eased in some while and she started playing with my fingers. The highway was getting dark and lonely and I needed to concentrate on road, so I shared my concern with her and she let me concentrate on road. We drove in silence till we reached outskirts of Bengaluru and hit the traffic snarls again.

She shifted on her seat and was sitting diagonally facing me. I could feel her facing me, so I looked at her for an instant and back at road, "What shonu?"

"What we had today was something special"

She paused for a moment expecting me to complete her sentence, but instead I preferred to respond in smile. So she continued, "but shouldn't we had waited for the marriage" "in that instant were you able to think?" I questioned her back in soft voice

"no"

"exactly!!" I thought I had proved my point, "It happened just because our emotions were running high and our love was stronger than conscience"

"then we have to keep your emotions in check till we get married"

"and why so?" I protested

"Because I say so" she told firmly

"If you didn't like my love for you, I don't have anything more to say" I played the guilt card

"I never said that"

"Then what was your meaning?"

She hesitated to speak, but then she finally spoke in a slow voice, "I love you and you make me crazy"

I placed my left hand around her chin and gave a small pinch on her cheek. "So?" I still tried to play dumb

"When you touch me, I feel shivers down my spine and I loose complete control of myself. And I am scared because of this?"

"Scared!!!"

"I have never loved anyone so much, and this is scary"

"Why Shonu?"

"The love part or the control part"

"Control part Sweetu"

"I don't know." And she kept her head on my shoulders. I placed a soft pat on her head and continued driving. I spoke a while later, " I have a confession to make"

"What confession? Is it something serious?" she asked. Her voice was scared. It was the first time after we met that I could see negative thoughts crossing her mind

"I will tell you when we reach home"

"No tell me now"

"I cant. I want to tell it when I can look straight into your eyes. It's a confession and no casual talk"

"I don't care. Tell me now" she was getting more scared and I could see signs of her getting hysterical.

So I parked the car in the first possible spot by the side of road, turned left towards her and took her hands in mine. I took a deep breath and then spoke, "I have had a lot many bad relationships in past. I used to walk off a relationship as soon as I sensed something wrong. I was a coward. Many times it was good that I walked off. But frankly I never felt love in any of those relationships. They were hollow emotions. Then I met you. You were pretty and cute. But the more I knew you, I fell in love with you. You are the most beautiful woman I have ever met. You are so positive, intelligent, full of energy and perfectly blended for me that you complete me. I love you my dear and dream of spending a life with you. Our official marriage may be a few months away, but mentally I think I have accepted you as my wife and want to treat you as one. You deserve that respect from me. And will never do anything to hamper that. I need you to trust me back the same way I trust you"

She started crying. I picked her face in my palms, rubbed off her tears, and asked why is he crying

"I know that sweetu, and hence it is scary. I cannot imagine a life without you."

"That's good na. Don't imagine anything. Just walk with me and we will make our life beautiful"

A little smile emerged on her lips while she tried to rub off her tears. She held my upper arm and rested her head on my shoulders again. I kissed her forehead and started again for her home.

When finally we reached her building, we went to Shubho's house to return his car keys and to thank them. Ruchi looked at Ankana. Her eyes were red and swollen and her voice was heavy with post cry effect. Ruchi looked at me, and said "She is my responsibility here, and I would prefer that you don't make her cry. ". Me and Ankana looked at each other with a smile, and Ankana replied, "I did cry because of this duffer, but not because he made me cry. I cried because of happiness"

"Don't fool me. I know you are taking his side. No one cries for happiness"

"No no. He is very good. And I cried because I couldn't handle all his love to me at once"

I stood there by the door with a big blush across my face. Ruchi also would have had such time in her life and so she could correlate. It was already very late in night so we took excuse and I went ahead to drop Ankana at her door. A few emotional looks and a couple of good bye kisses later I left for my home. In the parking, Shubho and Ruchi were standing next to my bike. Shubho twitched my ears, while Ruchi spoke, "She is a very sweet girl and I will kill you if you harm her or make her cry again. Do whatever you want after marriage, but before that you have to go by my rule book"

"I know it. And let me reassure you I am in love and I care more about her than what you can ever" and I gave a sarcastic smile to Ruchi

"Better that be true, young man" said Shubo. He continued with a smile, "I don't want anyone to mess with my wife's orders"

Ruchi said, "I am happy to know you are taking this relationship seriously"

"I have to. I can never find a better girl than Ankana" I replied.

A few small discussions later I left for home. By the time I reached home I had multiple messages on phone from Ankana. The first one read, "It took me long but my heart loves you, my eyes adore you, my mind respects you and I want to touch you, just to make sure you are real". The rest of the messages said the same thing in different way. I immediately called her and we spoke continuously till Sunday morning.

The cracks in the foundation

Next few days I could see a different Ankana. She was continuously giggling, smiling and chirping like a bird. She was glowing with happiness. She couldn't keep her hands off me. She kissed me on my face and my hands at every possible instant. She was definitely at an emotional high. At times it was awkward too, but I could understand her emotions. I knew I needed to talk to her and get her emotions channelized. I had to calm her down. I had to make her realize that I will be there for her for rest of life and she needed to accept the fact and check her emotions.

I was avoiding a direct talk to her, as I knew that could be interpreted in all possible negative ways. Her emotions could be brittle. So instead I stayed at her home one night, and let her sleep holding me. My trick worked and she did feel content and confident. She understood that I was there for her and would keep her safe. She did calm down to quite an extent.

The next few weeks, it became a daily affair. We used to spend evenings together cuddled in the couch and on few occasions for the whole night. I understood that it was a phase where the trust develops and the relationship stabilizes. It was new for me as well. I was showing restraint and kept myself in check. Her touch being the most amazing thing, required lot of effort on my side to keep things in check. She on the other hand was getting used to being in love.

At my personal front, I was no longer speculating whether I can win my lady or not. I knew she was mine and I was hers. And this showed in our interactions. I didn't have to prove anyone that we were in a relationship. Our relationship had definitely matured. Or was it just my thought. Every relationship as it matures, in a due course it develops lot of expectations and so did ours. And I didn't realize that. It never occurred to me that our relationship was in a stage where the high emotions do create signals of fragility.

This started with the small get together she organized on a weekend for her fellow teachers in the school. She wanted them to meet me. I bought some flowers and reached her home early that day to help her with the preparations and hosting. It was quite evident that she wanted me on her side while she did preparations for the get together. Because of frequent night stays, I had a couple of cloths in her house. I quickly put on one of them and joined her in the kitchen.

We were half way through in our preparations when the doorbell rang. A couple of her colleagues had arrived early to help her with preparations. Quickly I changed onto my formal cloths and invited them in. We were actually surprised to have them so early. I let the ladies take over the kitchen, while I changed flowers in the vase. Later I cleaned up the dining table and took out the serving crockeries from the wooden cabinet. The ladies were frolicking, but I didn't pay much attention at first. But when their laughter increased, I looked at Ankana. She was blushing and her face had turned red. Her colleagues were high on wits. I knew it must have been about me, otherwise she was humorous enough to counter their wits. I quietly pulled up a chair and placed it outside the kitchen facing all of them. They at first didn't notice me, but soon they became cautious with their comments.

To break the ice, I said, "She is a darling, and my princess. Please direct your comments this side and leave her alone". The trick worked and they opened up with me as well. I was very calculative with my answers. I hadn't opened up with them as I would do with my gang of friends. As more guests arrived the energy of the room also increased. I was the lone male in a gang of ladies. Some of them were friendly and they sat with me around the dining table. The jealousy and possessiveness forced Ankana to leave the kitchen and come and stand behind me. We were in love and it was obvious. And it gave the ladies more topics to make fun about us. Ankana had been working continuously in kitchen for hours, so I asked her to sit down, but she was eager to stand behind me with her arms wrapped around me. I turned and swiftly pulled her by her waist and made her sit on my lap. This action pulled all eyes on us, and everyone in a synchronization called out, "OOOhhh la la la". Ankana dug her face onto my chest because of shyness. I placed a soft kiss on her head. This was followed by a series of Bollywood style comments and romantic songs.

We had nothing to do other than smile back at them, look at each other and talk with eyes. To our rescue the doorbell rang again, and walked in three ladies with two young kids. I found one of them familiar, but couldn't place her at first. I let the ladies enjoy the get together, and I took the kids inside her bedroom. But my mind was still trying to put a name to that familiar face. While I was playing with the kids, a few eyes pried onto us from the living room. One of them was that of the familiar face. I did feel awkward but was not able to place her in my past.

Ankana walked into the room, pulled the cheeks of the kids and waved my hair. The food was ready and it was time to gorge onto it. She took us to the living room, where some ladies were sitting, some standing, some drinking coke and Fanta, but all had one thing in common. All eyes were on me. In a defensive action, I placed my hands around Ankana's waist, and pulled her in front of me, as if I was hiding

behind her. Before Ankana could say anything, I said, "It has been many years that so many teachers have their eyes convicting me. I have changed over the years. Believe me whatever it is, I am not the culprit" and then I looked at Ankana, "Please save me". Everyone burst out in laughter, Ankana punched on my chest, kissed me on my lips and turned towards them. "Well he is crazy, he is mad, he is an idiot. But whatever he is, he has my heart. And I love him and will marry him and only him. Let me introduce you all to Daksh, my fiancé. "

She then led me by hands and introduced me to each one of them. When she introduced that familiar face as Urmi, it dawned on me. Though I kept my expressions as genuine as possible, I didn't allow Ankana to get a feeling that Urmi was one face from my past. When I was new in the city, and roaring to enjoy my new found independence, I had met this lady in one late night party at a pub. She was high and she passed out with her arms around me. Since I didn't know her address, I carried her with me to my home. In the morning when she woke up, she was angry on me. She did think I must have used her while she was not in her senses. But after a cup of black coffee, when her senses were back, she thanked me for not leaving her alone in the party after she had passed out. Over the next few hours we did hit off and became friends. Later in the evening, I dropped her home. She invited me to her home for dinner, and I had agreed. We sat down to watch a movie while we had wine. During a romantic scene in the movie, she turned towards me, and asked, so what is wrong in that scene? I was a little embarrassed to be watching a love making scene sitting in a girl's home whom I had known less than 24 hours. And the specific question was an added embarrassment. I spilled wine out of my mouth, looked at her, and asked "why are you asking it?"

She said "just wanted to know if you know how to please a woman"

I was dumbstruck. I couldn't respond, I couldn't even blink my eye. She jumped on me, her hands in my hair, and her lips on mine. Before I could realize she had taken off her clothes and was un-doing my trouser. It was awkward, but the way she was kissing my ears and neck, it was erotic. I did lose control over self and picked her up in my arms and took her to her bedroom. We made love.

The next three days we stayed at her home only. We watched movies, ordered food, had lots of wine and beer, and made lot of love. She was a student of human psychology. But I had an office to attend to, and hence I took leave to attend office. But evenings we used to meet again mostly at her house for next couple of weeks. It was like I was in a magic spell. My friends found my nature changed, I looked tired and deprived of sleep. So one day Armaan took me to his home, where he

made sure I slept early and late into the morning. In the morning I saw a missed call from her, and when I called her back she didn't pick up. That evening when I went to her home, she wasn't there, and she didn't pick her phone. I was worried for her, and tried reaching her for next couple of days. Finally she had messaged me "Please stop calling me". That evening I went to meet at her home, just to find her with some other man. I walked out with no other word spoken. I was young and had made a big mistake. Actually it was a mistake which led to a big learning. The short but intense physical relationship was over as sudden as it had started.

Over the years I had forgotten her. But now she was back as a colleague of Ankana. Her eyes were gazed on me. She was carrying a plastic smile in the party, and I knew she remembered me as well. I didn't want to tell Ankana about her or my past with her, as I was not sure of her reaction. I didn't know how she would take it. And given the fact that Ankana and me were planning to get married, it didn't bother to me who stands around us. Ankana had all my attention.

The party was a success and we had a name by the end of it "C cube". It was an acronym for Cute and Crazy Couple. Once they all left, I sighed a big breath of relief, and she came running in my arms with a kiss on my lips. She closed her eyes and stood there holding me for a while. When she opened her eyes, she had a big smile on her face. She ruffled my hair and said a long "thankyouuuuuuuuu". We crashed on the sofa, with her head on my lap. The rest of the evening we watched television.

When she went back to school, her colleagues had all great words about us as a couple and how we complete each other and made for each other. She kept on messaging me the exact comments by them at every instant all through the day. I was happy because she was happy. She was in her happiest best. She was in her dreamland. She was mad in love, and so was I. I also wanted to break all inhibitions and shout out to the world that I was in love, but my true love had made me shy.

A few days later I got a call in the evening. It was an unknown number. Before I could pick it up it disconnected. A few minutes later the same number called again and hanged up. This went on for some time more. I messaged at that number – "Who is this?"

Immediately that number called back again, and I picked it up at the first ring. I shouted back, "Who is this?"

I could hear a suppressed smile at the other end. A few long breaths later the lady on other end spoke, "why are you so eager to know who I am"

"I am not eager. I am irritated by your continuous missed calls" I was angry

"I thought you will recognize me"

"Sorry I don't know you"

"No one has ever forgotten me"

I really got pissed off. "If you want to identify yourself, do it. Or else I am hanging up"

"Don't tell me you have forgotten the nights you spent with me?"

"Which nights? With whom?" I was really pissed off.

"Don't sound so ignorant"

That was it. Without saying anything further, I just hanged up. She tried calling me a couple of more times, but I didn't pick up. I did cool down a bit and I was a bit scared. My life was perfect, and if statistics are to be believed that was quite unlikely.

As Ankana had other plans later that evening, I preferred to have an early night. When I woke up in the morning, a message was waiting on my Inbox, "The way your eyes looked at me in the party, I know they want to see more". It felt as if I was dealing with a psychopath.

I tried to ignore it, but then while brushing my teeth, I looked at myself in the mirror and my past flashed across my eyes. The feeling that I may have unintentionally crossed someone's path in a bad way made me feel guilty. But then the question about who I hurt and why she wants to harass me when I am happy, got me thinking. It dawned on me that the message talked about a party, and the only party I had been in past few days was at Ankana's place. And instantly I had a name for the alleged psychopath. It had to be Urmi.

I was now less scared once I knew the identity, but the bigger fight self within was whether to tell Ankana about this or not. Also what I didn't understand was how Urmi got hold of my phone number.

My phone received another message, "Hope you read my message. How did I look in your dream?"

I tried to ignore it initially but then I thought otherwise and I replied, "I know who you are and you were never in my life"

Instantly a reply came, "If I wasn't how you did know me?"

Better sense prevailed, and I stopped myself from replying. I preferred to ignore her, as my responses would only get her more of what she wanted.

The next few days, I kept getting missed calls and occasional dirty messages, but I preferred to ignore them, and kept continuing living as usual. But at back of my head, I was not at ease. The messages were getting more personal every passing day and had details of my present day personal information as well. It was as if she was around me, and was keeping a vigil eye on me every day. All I wanted was to marry Ankana and live in peace. I didn't want my past to be a bottleneck to this. And Urmi was turning out to be a real psychopathic case. But I was still not sure how did she get my number and how did she know so much about me.

Continuous messages and missed calls were taking effect on my personal conduct. I was not at my usual being. Infact Ankana pointed out my change of behavior, and was worried about me. I kept on telling her that everything was fine, but that was a big lie. I didn't want her to get tensed. I wanted to handle my past and everything related to it my way.

One weekend afternoon, when we had nothing to do, Ankana and I were watching a movie on television. In way of casual talk I asked her, "So how is school?"

"Its good. And after our get together lunch party, everyone has become very friendly"

"Oh is it. That's good na"

"Yeah its good, but very awkward to be true"

"Why awkward?"

"There is no boundary at times. They keep asking personal stuffs which I am not very keen to share. They want to know intimate details about us. And some of them keep digging facts about you. You only tell isn't this awkward?"

"Yeah true it is. But why they want to ask about me or stuffs about us. Why is their talk limited to you?"

"I don't know. Sometimes I feel insecure."

"Insecure about?"

"Why are they taking so much interest about you and our relationship?"

I kissed on her forehead gently, "You don't have to be. I am all yours and will not let you off my arms" and I tightly hugged her in my arms.

A few minutes later, with a blink in my eye, I asked, "Achcha what do they ask about me?"

She punched softly on my chest, and looked innocently into my eyes, "do you really want to know?"

"But obviously. When we grow old, we will remember these things and have a hearty laugh. But if you don't tell me this now, you will take some good moments away from our old age"

She smiled, thought a bit, "You know Smita was asking about your home city, your schooling and all. Harsha was asking about your office address. And this Urmi seems especially interested in you."

My shock was visible through my eyes. She continued, "Earlier she never spoke to anyone and behaved as if her working as a teacher was a big compliment for the betterment of society. But recently she is very friendly with me. She has lunch and tea always with me. She keeps on asking about our relationship, where we met, how it started, what we talk, and almost every possible thing that can be asked. She even asked for your phone number."

Instantly I blurted out, "And you gave her? You shouldn't have given"

She looked at me with surprise, but continued, "No I didn't, but the other day she took my mobile and started playing some games in it. I went to wash my hands, and when I came back, she was browsing my contacts. I took my phone back, but I doubt she must have gone through my messages as well. Now I keep my phone always with me."

"Oh my God. That was too much of peeking into personal space. And she sounds like a psycho. Try keeping a distance from her" I suggested

"yeah that's what even I was thinking"

We did change the topic of discussion, but I knew where Urmi got my number from. Also from Ankana's reactions I knew she didn't like her as well.

That very Monday, Urmi called. I didn't pick her call. But when she kept on calling continuously, I had to pick up, "If you think by stopping Ankana from talking to me will save you, you are wrong. You just made my resolve even stronger"

"What the hell do you want? Why can't you leave us alone?" I was really angry.

"I want you back. I have searched you long, but couldn't. When I saw you with Ankana, you reminded me of those days when we were all over each other."

"How disgusting you are."

She let out a long laugh, a laugh indicating arrival of bad things.

I cut the call. I was tensed. I didn't want her around me or Ankana. She was indeed a big threat for our relationship. I knew Ankana had to be involved. So that evening I went to her home. She was very quiet, but her eyes were angry.

"I want to talk something very important. But it seems you are not in a good mood."

"From when have you started caring about my mood?"

Her reaction was shocking but then I continued, "When have I not done that?"

"If not then why did you hide facts from me?"

"What did I hide?"

"May be hundreds of things, but let start with Urmi"

"I came to talk about that only"

"But obviously this will be your excuse now. Why didn't you tell earlier? What is so special today?"

"Because I didn't expect her to be an issue, but I see her now as a psycho case who wants to ruin our relationship"

"Don't put blame on her. I know you are not able to keep yourself in control."

"Is that what you think? You don't have any trust on me?"

"I had but now I doubt it"

I was pissed off, but I couldn't reply back to her. I was broken from within. All what I ever wanted was to be happy with Ankana ever after, and hence was keeping my past away from my present. But just a small thing had taken her trust away from me.

I walked over to balcony and stood there quietly. My world had shown the initial cracks. I was scared. My beautiful world had begun to fall apart.

Almost ten minutes later, I walked in to a crying Ankana. She was sitting on the floor by the sofa. I sat next to her and tried to hold her by her shoulders. I wanted to calm her down, but she shrugged me off. I shifted to sit in front of her, facing her. I tried to wipe off her tears but she pushed me away. I didn't know what to do, so I just sat there. It must have been hours we sat like that, she crying out of control and me sitting quietly looking at her. Finally her eyes dried out, and she could control her emotions, "You came to tell something. Tell it quickly and then go home"

"It was for our sweet home, I didn't tell anything about her earlier"

"No need to give dialogues."

I took a long breath, "When I looked at her in the party, initially I couldn't recollect her. But I knew she was a part of my past. A past which I cannot change, but which I regret. From the day I have met you, all what I have wanted is a future with you. I have been ashamed of my past and have been really scared that my past may take you away from me." I stopped for a while to recollect myself, "Then when you introduced her to me, I could place her in my life when I was new in this city and was young and immature. We had met in a pub, and because she had passed out over me while dancing, I had taken her to my home as I didn't know her address. The next day when she woke up, we got introduced, and when I went to drop off her home, our young energy converged and followed with a physical relationship for a couple of weeks, before one day suddenly she found another man and I was out of her life. I felt as I was used, but then I moved ahead in life."

She was quietly listening to me, while I continued, "After the party, she somehow got hold of my number and started giving me blank calls and then bad messages. Initially I didn't know who she was. I initially thought her of a psychopath stalker, but soon realized she was her, and that she wants to break us and instead have a relationship with me."

She waited a while after I was done, as if weighing her words, "But if I believe you, why didn't you tell me earlier. Why did you hide facts from me. "

"I was myself tensed as I didn't know the identity. I didn't want to get you also tensed. But then when I came to know of her identity, I thought I can get away from my past myself. Frankly I was scared that you will judge me on my past." As she didn't speak anything I continued, "But today she called and started shouting that I have asked you to be away from her. And then she said she will replace you in my life. When I scolded her, she gave a very scary laugh. I was scared for you and hence I came to talk to you"

She kept quietly staring into me. "But do you know Daksh, she did mention something else to me"

"What?"

"That she called you to congratulate you and catch over the past, but then you tried to flirt with her and asked her out"

"that's rubbish"

"I don't know whom to trust?"

"Will you trust her or me? For god sakes we are getting married in a few months, and you are not trusting me"

"I have my doubts Daksh"

I took out my phone and let her read all her messages. I also showed that I never called her and it was she who always gave me a call. I begged her to believe me. Her heart was finally taking over her head and I could see the belief develop again for me in her eyes. Finally she gave me a big hug and spoke softly in my ears, "you are all I have got. And I know you had a past, but then you have to understand, I cannot even think of sharing you for a moment with anyone. Please be mine" and she started crying again.

I held her face just in front of mine, wiped off her tears and said, "I love you, and you are what I have got."

She punched me hard on my chest, smiled a bit and said, "I am hungry"

I looked at my watch, it was past midnight. I quickly walked to the kitchen and prepared noodles. After that I tucked her in the bed and she slept off instantly. Whole night I lay there on the couch with my eyes open. This was our first fight and I was scared. I was giving everything I had got to this relationship, but was not able to stop the cracks getting developed. If it had been any of my earlier relationships I would have walked off without a second thought, but with Ankana it was different. I was in love and I was eager to settle. She was all I had got and I couldn't imagine anything without her.

In morning I prepared her breakfast, and then later dropped her to her school. I did ask her to keep a distance from Urmi and not discuss anything. Ankana did promise me that. I took the day off, and wanted to catch on some sleep so I went home. Later in the morning, Urmi sent me a message, "I know you two fought yesterday over me. I know we will be a couple very soon"

I didn't reply anything back to her but forwarded that message instantly to Ankana. I wanted to keep her included. I didn't get any reply from her and neither did I get anything from Urmi. That afternoon I went to pick up Ankana from school. She was angry, her eyes suggested she had cried again. But I didn't say anything before we reached her home. Once inside, I stood in front of her, tucked her hair behind her ears, and angled her face towards mine. But her eyes were looking down. I quietly asked, "What *Shonu*?"

She took some time before she spoke, "She said that you lust for her and that she will have sex with you this weekend"

I couldn't help but a laugh came out. She looked puzzled at me, "Was that funny?"

I checked my laugh, "No it was not. But to know from someone else what I think and what I am going to do is definitely not normal"

"Tell me what she said is not true"

"Do I have to now advocate for myself?"

"Yes"

I could sense the emotional turmoil she was going through, so in a very serious tone I said, "I love you and the only person I will ever have sex in my life is only with my wife, and that is you"

"But we are yet not married"

"So what. I have told you earlier as well. You are the only one I am getting married to, and I look at you as my wife"

She clinched my hands, tried to give a smile and sat down in the couch. I sat next to her. I asked "But why did you talk to her?"

"I didn't want to, but after you forwarded her message, I confronted her. She said bad words to me, and challenged me. In retaliation I pulled off her hairs and slapped her"

I kissed her on her cheeks, and in a very soft voice spoke next to her ears, "My wild cat"

She pushed me down on couch, kept her head on my shoulders and lied down on top of me. I laid there quietly allowing her to absorb the moment and stabilize her emotions.

Rest of the week, I dropped her to school, picked her up from school and after dinner only left back for my home.

Saturday morning, my doorbell rang. Half asleep I opened my door with sleepy eyes. It was Urmi. She pushed her way in. My eyes turned wide open in a split second. I knew why she was at my home. She had challenged Ankana earlier that week and she had come to prove her point.

The first thing that crossed my mind was to call Ankana. I rushed to my bedroom where I had kept my phone. Urmi closed the main door and followed me, and pinned me down on bed even before I could reach for my cellphone. I slapped her hard, and tried to push her away from me. But her hold was strong. She stared down at me, "There was a time when you couldn't keep your hands off me, and pants on your waist. And now you act like a saint?"

"That was many years ago. Times have changed and so have I"

"But I haven't and nor your feelings for me."

"Get off me"

"I cant keep away from you", and she tore my shirt and started kissing my neck and chest. I kept trying pushing her off, but she was heavy. The door bell rang, and at that instant I could push her and stood up. While walking to the door, I removed my torn shirt. I opened the door bare chested to see Ankana. She was standing there with a big smile.

Urmi stepped out from bedroom and in front of the open door. She had an evil smile on her face. Ankana's smile gave way to horror in her eyes. She didn't say a word, just turned and walked away down the stairs.

I shouted, "it is not what it looks like"

She didn't utter a word, just walked off. I ran behind Ankana asking her to stop. But by the time I could reach downstairs, she had left. I stood there barefoot only in my boxers. People looked at me, and I looked at the empty road. It felt as if my world had fallen apart. My mind was not working. I was still. I had no life in my limbs.

A while later Urmi walked down still flashing the evil smile. She stood in front of me, "Now she is gone forever. And you have no one other than me"

In that moment, I gave her a tight slap on her cheeks turning them into red. "I am only for Ankana" and I ran back upstairs. I had to be with Ankana. I put on a shirt and a pair of Jeans and rode back to her home.

Anger

When I reached her door, it was locked from outside. She hadn't reached home. I ran down to Shubho's house. His house was also locked from outside. I tried calling her, but neither did she pick up the calls, nor did she call back. I left her numerous messages, but no response. I didn't know where else to find her, so I sat outside her apartment door and preferred to wait for her. Deep down I was scared for her well-being. I didn't know where to find her. She needed to know the truth. I was only for her. I didn't do anything wrong.

While I was in my thoughts, Ruchi called, "What has happened between you two again?"

"Did she call you now?"

"Yes she did"

"Where is she?"

"She said she is fine, and wants to be left alone"

"She is not answering my calls"

"Did you two have a fight?"

"No. Actually much more than that?"

"What do you mean? Anyways where are you?"

"Waiting for her upstairs"

"Come down. We will reach home in 5 minutes"

I was waiting for them at their door. I looked devastated. I had just pulled up a pair of jeans and a t-shirt and rode back to her house in a hurry. My hair was unkept, my stubble looked dirty and I was bare foot. I went inside, took some time to collect myself, but told them about each and every fact about the Urmi fiasco.

After listening to all, Shubho said with a sarcastic smile, "Urmi really did that?"

I stared back at him. I was in no mood of jokes. Ruchi interrupted, "For Gods sake

Shubho, this is serious. Ankana is a very simple girl. For the first time she is in love. A new relationship is based on trust, but what happened today was something that will definitely leave a scar for long." She looked at me "Your stars are not in correct position."

Shubho turned serious, "I was just trying to lighten up the tension." He took a pause, and then said, "My first concern here is to find Ankana and bring her back home"

Ruchi immediately called her and asked her whereabouts. She kept the call, asked me to stay back and asked Shubho to come. They went in their car to bring her back. I waited impatiently.

Half an hour later they came with Ankana. Her eyes were swollen and her tears had dried. She must have cried for hours. She looked down at me with angry eyes. "What is he doing here?" she asked Ruchi.

I wanted to plead my innocence. I moved towards her. She raised her hands asking me to stop where I was. She continued, "She proved her point. She challenged me and she won"

"No she didn't. "

"Quiet Daksh. Don't give excuse. I saw with my eyes"

"That's not true Sweetu"

"I am not your Sweetu. May be she is. Go to her"

"Why are you talking like this?"

"Why am I? You don't know?" she was angry

"I didn't do anything. I was resisting"

"Yeah and I am a liar"

"No you are not"

"Exactly"

"But she came down with an agenda"

"Oh so she is the leopard and you are the dear"

"Exactly what I am trying to say"

She gave me a long stare, "For once I assured myself that you had left your past behind. That you are a changed man. All your friends too pitched in your favor. But my fault. How could I trust you. You were never mine. You can never change. You will always be a spineless horny man. And I can never have a happy future with you. Your past will always hunt you down."

"You are overreacting" I replied in a hysterical raised voice

"The truth hurts. Isn't it?"

"Why are you not understanding? This is not the truth"

She kept her finger on her lips, and in a hand action asked me to stay quiet. After a deep breath she said, "Your past ruined our future."

I stood their motionless. Every word resonating loud between my ears. Tears formed in the corner of my eyes. I couldn't believe what I heard. I wanted to hug her, and assure her that she was my only priority and our future was together. She was the one for me. I was no longer the older being. All I cared was her. I stepped towards her with my spread arms.

She stepped back, "Don't even try. I don't even want to see you" She turned towards Ruchi, "I am going to my house. Make sure this guy leaves directly from here. I don't want to see him." And she walked out of their house.

We all stood there. I tried going behind her, but Shubho held my arms. Ruchi closed the main door behind Ankana, and walked over to stand in front of me. "She is really angry. And it won't do any good if you talk to her now. Let her calm down. Give it a couple of days. Let us talk to her. You just go back home, and wait"

"But.." I protested

"Believe us" she assured me.

I sat down on their couch with my head between my hands. I couldn't believe the turn of events. Till yesterday she was all mine, she was my princess. And now everything had changed.

Shubho quickly prepared me a cup of tea. We all sat for a while in silence. I was trying to sink in the day. But the day was much bigger than that. After a while I rose and walked towards the main door with stooped shoulders, to return home. It seemed like I was drained out of all my energy. Looking at me, Shubho decided to

accompany me to my home and stayed with me for the night.

I slept late in the night. Till very late I was sitting by the corner of the bed with millions of thoughts crossing my mind. I sent a few messages to Ankana. I knew she was awake, but she didn't reply to either of them. It was the longest night and seemed to have no end, but eventually sometime within that night, I dozed off.

In the morning I woke up with an urgency. I picked up my phone and called Ankana. She cut my call. It hurt. But the good thing was that she atleast responded in a way. The previous day she was just letting it ring. It was not a good feeling at all, but I was desperately looking for an opportunity to talk to her. I knew if I can hold her hand, she will get my warmth and true feeling for her. I couldn't do it the previous day in Shubho and Ruchi's presence.

I quickly got off the bed and rushed to get fresh. Shubho came out of Living room to find me getting ready. "Now where are you going?"

"To Ankana"

"I don't think that will be a good idea. As we told yesterday, she is going through a lot of emotions man. Give her some personal time. Don't pound on her and don't nag her right now. Leave her alone"

"But" I protested

"No. Just listen to me" he told in a stern voice while holding my shoulders square

I didn't want to listen to him, but I trusted him. My shoulders drooped again and my energy again vanished. I sat down on the bed. In a desperation I called out, "I will kill this Urmi. She is the culprit"

"No you won't do anything. Just ignore Urmi"

"That bitch spoiled everything."

"Nothing has been spoiled. Just avoid Urmi, and no contact with her whatsoever."

"She will repent her actions"

"Daksh you are not listening"

"Yeah yeah yeah"

"What was that?"

"Nothing"

"Listen, you are not in your senses. You are not thinking properly. Just don't do anything that you will repent later" he paused, then continued "better just don't do anything. Just keep your words inside your mouth and thoughts inside your skull"

I looked at him with disgust and frustration. He replied "Just don't. Trust me"

He then pulled me up and said 'Come lets go out and have some breakfast. You need something in your stomach"

During breakfast, he diverted topic to some news in print media. We took our time in breakfast but when we came back, I was much stable emotionally. Shubho seeing that I was in control of self, left back for his home with an assurance that he will personally talk to Ankana.

A while later Armaan called me. He was making a plan with his office colleague for a long drive and wanted to check if I was willing to join. He was not aware of what had happened the previous day. He did sense something amiss in my voice, and on his enquiry I told him the complete incident. He heard it all very quietly. When I was done, he said, "Really?"

I said "what?"

"She sat on top of you and tore off your shirt"

"That's what you made out of the complete incident"

"No no. I stopped at that description only. I was busy visualizing it. It must have been.."

I cut him off, "It's no time for jokes *yaar*"

"Man, who is joking. I am damn serious. I want to be the man under her. Wish it was her shirt that was torn"

"Armaan" I literally shouted out his name in disgust and anger

"ok ok.. chill.. You are over thinking it all. Ankana is just upset, and in couple of days you two love birds will again be in each other's arm"

I just replied with a "hmmm" sound. He wished me all the best and continued for his long drive. He promised to be with me the next day evening after office hours.

A few minutes later, Shubho called to let me know that Ruchi spoke to Ankana and was with her the previous night. Ankana was feeling very low, and she decided to visit her parents. She left for Kolkata in the afternoon flight. Hearing this I was filled with burning anger within me. How could she go back and not even tell me. I kept my thoughts to me, and didn't let Shubho know about my anger. I just responded with "OK. Thanks man for letting me know"

As soon as I cut the call, I punched hard on the wall to let out my anger. I took out whiskey and poured myself a glass. It followed with a couple of more glasses before the doorbell rang. My steps were swinging. I opened the door to find Urmi. She pushed me aside and forced herself in.

"As soon I came to know that she left for Kolkata, I knew things are not good between both of you right now. I just came to tell you that you are not alone. I am with you"

The first thought that crossed my head was, how she knew that Ankana left for Kolkata. But I blurted out, "It's all because of you"

"Let's not play blame game. Instead let's utilize the opportunity. No one will come between us now. We can finish off what we started yesterday"

In an instant, I was taken over by anger, and shouted back at her "You nymphomaniac"

She instead responded with a smile and came closer to me, "isn't that good for you?" and she pushed me to the wall.

I held her chin with a tight grip and pushed her back. But she kept coming on me. Rage was completely taking over me. In a sudden move I held her shirt by the top and tore it off. She gave out a happy sigh "Finally". I pinned her down to the bed. She had a smile on her face and her hands were keeping me close to her. I unbuttoned her jeans and jerked it off. She bent forward to take off my shirt, at which moment I turned her by her arms and held her tight while she lay there on her stomach. My hold on her arms was tight and she cried out in pain. My eyes were searching around for something, and I got hold of a pillow. I took out the pillow cover, rolled it vertically and tied her hands by her back. I turned her over. Her smiling face was now covered with doubts. I walked to my cupboard, and brought my belt back to tie her legs by the ankle. I held her by chin and pulled her up to a standing position, pulled her to the corner of the room. She was scared now. She called out a loud cry for help, at which moment I gave her a tight slap on her left cheek. I could see blood changing color of her skin.

Her fair cheek turned red along the mark of my slap. My head was paining a bit and I was filled with rage. I was not in my senses,

"Shhhhhhh" I called out with my fingers on my lips

She stood there with scared eyes, her body covered only in revealing undergarments and she feeling completely uncomfortable. I held her with her neck. With a bit of effort I controlled my words and said, "What we had years back is called youth. We had a great time but then we moved ahead in life. I have forgotten you and have no interest whatsoever left. I love Ankana. I love her madly. Finally I have found the purpose of my life. And you walk in into my world trying to destroy it." My head was now throbbing with pain. I punched hard on my temple and slapped myself to be conscious. I was struggling. Alcohol was controlling me. I pointed my fingers at her breast, "You come here with this and try to lure me. What do you think of me? Am I characterless? No I am not. Only Ankana has the right over me, and no one else. Is that clear?"

She nodded her head in affirmative, while her eyes still in terror.

"Look yourself in the mirror', I pointed to the mirror in the room "Don't you feel ashamed in this state with an unknown man. You will have five or may be ten years left with a youthful body. Then age will start taking over. You will be no different than anyone else. Stop using your body now, or else you will die alone in shame and regret. Find a decent man and settle with him. Devote yourself to a family." I took a pause and with lot of emphasis shouted "Leave Ankana and me alone for God's sake"

I left my hold on her and turned around. Before I could realize I fell on the floor and I passed out.

I woke up to a series of doorbell. I gathered myself up, and opened the door. It was morning. Armaan was standing there with a concerned look, "Why are you not picking up your phone?"

I rubbed my eyes, "when were you calling?" my head still heavy.

"I called you in the night and then in the morning. You didn't answer so I came to check"

Armaan was by now in my living room. The whiskey bottle was kept on the table uncapped. He looked at me with questioning eyes while screwing back the cap, looking for an answer. I had no memory of the previous night. I asked him to sit, and went inside for restroom. As I walked in to my bedroom, I saw Urmi sitting in the corner. In a surprise I called out loud, "Oh shit". Armaan came running inside. She also saw Urmi. She had cried all night. She was looking back at us with guilt, fear, shame and pleading for a pity. Armaan slapped my shoulders, "Whats this Daksh?"

I had no idea what to reply. I looked back at his staring eyes which were not believing what it saw. I turned back towards Urmi, rushed to her, and untied hers arms and legs. Armaan pulled out my bedsheet in one swift action and covered her up.

I couldn't recollect what had happened. I was horrified. I sat in front of Urmi on my knees, "When did you come to my home and why are you tied like this? Did I do this to you? Did I do anything else to you?"

She looked at me with dead eyes and started crying out loudly. Armaan came and pushed me aside, pulled her up with a comforting hold around her shoulders, walked her to restroom "Compose yourself and get yourself clean."

She closed the door behind her, and Armaan came running to me, "Who is she? And what is she doing here?"

"She is Urmi and trust me I don't know what she is doing here"

"She is Urmi" he called out in a surprised tone "Man did you two have sex?" and before I could answer, "Ankana will kill you for this"

Urmi had walked back to the room to fetch her jeans and top. She replied, "No we didn't. He is Ankana's" and walked back inside.

I came out to living room with Armaan and sat down with head in my arms. I kept murmuring "Shit! Shit! Shit!". Armaan sat with a puzzled look

Urmi came out in a few minutes with shy steps. She was clearly uncomfortable. She was wearing the torn top and holding her at places to save her dignity. Armaan opened his bike jacket and wrapped it around her. She quickly zipped it up with a thanks to Armaan. She picked her purse and walked towards the exit door.

Armaan called out loud, "Hey Urmi, hold on" she stopped and turned towards Armaan. Armaan continued "I am Armaan. You may not know me. But I am the main reason your relationship didn't blossom years back. I thought you are a bad influence on him, and I made him forget you"

Urmi looked at him. She had no reaction. Her face was expressionless. Armaan continued "Now he is with Ankana and for once we find him serious in a relationship. Ankana is the best thing that can happen to him. And he also realizes that. But he is a confused soul on this earth. I don't know what you two have now or what you had yesterday. But it doesn't seem good at face value"

She didn't reply. I looked at her with questioning eyes. Her eyes met mine for a flash second. "I am sorry for tying you up. But I don't remember anything of the previous night" I said in a very sheepish voice.

She looked up at me and then while looking at Armaan she said "I did want him back in my life. When I saw him, he reminded me of my youth days. And I tried to win him back. But clearly he is Ankana's. I don't deserve a chance"

"But what happened yesterday" Armaan asked

"I tried to establish physical relation with him, instead he tied me up and gave me a lecture" she said in a sheepish voice without a pause looking down at the ground

"We didn't have sex right?" I jumped for that question

She stared long back at me "No" and then she walked out to leave.

Armaan and me called out a sigh together on hearing No. Armaan offered to drop her back home, but she declined and quietly walked out of home.

The Shit-hole

I couldn't concentrate in office the whole week. I dreamt of Ankana. Without her around I felt so lonely. My phone, office and personal laptop had Ankana as the desktop wallpaper now. My manager was constantly reminding me about the lack of my productivity in office. Every evening I used to send a message to Ankana, telling what she meant to me. But she never responded in any way. I even wrote her a few romantic letters.

I was expecting her to come back from home in a week, but she didn't. She didn't answer my calls, didn't reply my messages, and didn't reply my emails. What I learnt from Shubho is that Ruchi was talking to her every day, but Ankana was going through an emotional turmoil. So I kept peace with myself.

A few days later, when I went to meet Shubho in the evening, I saw light through Ankana's house window. I rushed straight up to her home, but there was no response to door bell. Ankana had a habit of breathing heavy whenever she had tears or was crying. I could hear the heavy breathing from other side of the door. But she didn't open the door. Instead Ruchi came running up. Ankana rather than opening door had called up Ruchi to come and take me away. I didn't want to go without talking to Ankana, but Ruchi held my hand and pulled me downstairs to her home. Ankana had come back the previous day, but she didn't tell me. I felt offended. Ankana was treating me as if I never existed. She had boycotted me completely. But unlike my previous relations, this time I was not ready to move on to someone else. I was hooked on to her. I was not ready to lose her. I was prepared to do anything to win her back.

Ruchi kept trying to console me and kept taking Ankana's side. Shubho also did not understand me. I got completely frustrated and left back for my home.

On reaching home I tried calling Ankana again. She didn't pick up as expected. So I left her a message "Don't even think that I am going to leave you. More you ignore me, more I will follow you"

Rest of the night I kept thinking of her. And more I thought of our good times, the more I got depressed knowing she was not with me at that moment. The whiskey bottle seemed like a good company, and I spent rest of the night drinking.

I went into depression over the next few days. Every evening I used to drink heavily. No one in my group knew this. Everyone was busy with their life and I didn't make my depression obvious.

One day late in the night Piyush got a call from my phone from an unknown person. He had dialed the person whom I had last spoken to.

"Do you know the owner of this number?"

"Yes. But who are you?" said Piyush

"Please come to Star Pub. Your friend is out of control and he needs someone to take him home"

Piyush called Armaan and both reached Star Pub. They found me sitting at the bar table, holding hands of a fellow customer. I was not letting him go. They heard me telling that person, "No Jaanu, you are more beautiful than Katrina. See your eyes, they are more appealing than of Madhuri. I don't want you to try in Bollywood. You will become famous, but I want you only for me". It seems I had been talking to that customer for over an hour, hallucinating him to be Ankana. Others were having a good time at the expense of my antiques.

It took them a lot of cajoling to take me back to Armaan's place. I woke up very late with a heavy head. Armaan had taken off from office, and was really pissed at me and my antiques. He was concerned that I had been on a self-destruction depressing mode. Once I was a bit sober and in my senses, he sat me across the dining table

"Ki korcho taa ki tumi?" (What are you doing man?) he said in a stern and angry tone

"Why what happened" I was clueless on what he was up to

"See yourself. You look and smell like a drunkard"

"Oh this. I just drank a bit more than usual" came my immediate response

"No I am not talking only of this incidence. We have been seeing you depressed lately. You nowadays don't come to meet us also. And when we meet you, you are not in your senses. Now we need to carry you back home as well. What have you done to yourself"

"Oh nothing.. Just that I am rethinking of my priorities"

"Good that you are rethinking. I do have a feeling that you have taken Ankana a bit too much to your heart"

"What do you mean?"

"I mean that in your previous instances, you would have walked out of relationships in a blink of eye. And here you are acting as devdas"

"No she is special" I protested

"In what way? Why is she special?"

"I don't know that. But she is. I want to get married to her"

"She was never yours Daksh. She was just another chapter in your life. The fact is that you were smitten by her beauty, but were never in love. You were just trying to justify your attraction for her as love"

"No you are not understanding Armaan. It's not like that. You won't understand"

"What will I not understand?"

"Nothing leave it"

"No tell me. Why are you destroying yourself for her?"

"I am not destroying myself"

"Yes you are Daksh. Just that you are not realizing that"

I took a moment of silence. Armaan's tone had concern and seriousness. May be he was correct. He instilled doubts in my mind. Ankana was still friends with my group and used to make sure to meet them only in my absence. She was not responding to my calls or messages. She was avoiding me. Maybe Armaan was correct. It was all just attraction. We were never meant to be together. But still my heart was not ready to accept that. I was sure that it was Love.

"No Armaan. I think it is a special connection"

"Think Daksh think. Take time and think seriously. It's your life. You are spoiling it"

"If you mean my drinking and all, I can assure you I will be in control and drink within my limits"

"Yes please do that. If possible don't drink at all"

I assured him again and then we went out for lunch. During lunch we hatched a plan to go for a long drive and trekking to Sakleshpura the next weekend. Piyush, Arpit and Shubho were also roped in. It was planned to be an all-boys outing. It took us a lot of negotiations to convince their better halves though.

That weekend was great. We re-lived our college days and we had loads of fun. It was a great opportunity for me to concentrate on something other than Ankana. I felt re-energized with positive energy, and after coming back, my work productivity in office also improved.

But then who can win over time and emotions. A few weeks later my positivity was gone and my energy was down. I kept myself busy with reading books, watching movies, playing games. I really tried hard to distract myself to not think about her. Some customer escalation had come in office, and I saw it as a good opportunity to get myself busy. I did a good job, but somehow my manager had other views. In a meeting he confronted me with his observations which I tried defending with logic. But it seemed he was hell bent to prove his point. I couldn't take further and our meeting turned to a heated argument. I walked out on him from the room, and the whole team watched.

In the evening I went out to a pub with an office colleague for a glass of beer. But emotions were running high. It felt as if the emptiness in my life because of Ankana, had come out as frustration on my manager. In a normal mindset I could have handled the situation better.

The discussions went on longer, and we had too much liquor. He got a call from his wife and he left for home. Alone my thoughts again drifted to Ankana. I was fed up with the feeling of emptiness. She had to get back in my life. I started thinking about my options to win her back.

An hour later, I was standing below her seventh floor balcony. I had a small local band with me, and a portable mic in my hand. The apartment security didn't allow me to enter, so I stood on the road outside the apartment wall. I called her at her cellphone, which she didn't pick. So at the highest possible voice I spoke at the mic "Ankana Ankana Ankana!!! You are a dream come true. You are what I have waited all my life. You complete me. You are my love, my life."

I saw her coming to the balcony and look down towards me. Looking at her after so many days, tears trickled down my eyes. I continued calling her name aloud "Ankana", "Ankana". I didn't notice the other residents also come out on their balcony. Some were amused, but most offended as I was breaking the peace of night.

Emotions took over me, and I started singing romantic Bollywood songs. With an unpleasant singing voice, I created a commotion in the neighborhood. Irritated people were coming out of their homes to figure out what was happening. In the meantime Shubho and Ruchi came running towards me. Their house was on the other side of the building, and I suppose Ankana would have informed them. They tried to stop me from singing and calm me down. But I was under the influence of alcohol. My voice went harsher and harsher, and the songs more irritating. I was surrounded by lot of depressed murmurs and some very high pitched curse words. A couple of men even came to physically handle me, but Shubho pacified them otherwise.

The whole commotion was broken with the sound of police siren. One inspector approached me with four constables following his lead. The band which was playing along me all this while, ran away at the very sight of police. Shubho tried to talk to the inspector, but he ignored him and ordered his constables to forcefully take me in the police jeep. They took away my mic and dragged me away. The inspector spoke to my mic requesting everyone to get back to their houses and assured them peace.

My eyes were continuously at Ankana who stood at the balcony. She was standing without any movement, and she didn't even move when police was dragging me away.

Shubho followed the police jeep to the police station. Armaan had also reached the police station by now. I had infact slept off on the way to station. I woke upto a splash of water thrown at my face. I was sitting in a chair in the middle of a cell, which had wall at one side and iron bars at other three. The inspector was sitting in front of me, and two constables standing by my side. I could see Shubho and Armaan peeking in through the iron bars.

"What hero, first you drink like this and then spoil the peace of the neighborhood. What do you think of yourself?" the inspector asked in a stern voice.

I looked back at him with blank eyes. I was still trying to understand the situation and my surroundings. But inspector moved forward and held my cheeks with a tight grip of his right hand, "I am asking something"

"She is not talking to me. I love her so much, but she is ignoring me" I replied in a hushed voice while trying to control my words

"Whom is he talking about" he asked turning to Shubho and Armaan. They preferred to keep quiet.

One of the constables replied instead, "Sir it's the same girl who called us and complained about him. She asked to come quickly and take him away. She was ashamed of his actions"

I stared at the constable. I couldn't believe him. The inspector gave me a tight slap instead, "What are you staring him for", he put a lot of emphasis on the word him. Then he started talking to the constable, "Nowadays this generation is like this only. They don't know what they are doing or whom they have feelings for. They just keep drifting. Seems his girl has also drifted away now. And this coward thinks he still has a chance." He stared back at me, "Forget her and move ahead. And if I see you near that apartment again, I swear to god, I will break your legs" he stood up and his chair moved back. He signaled Shubho and Armaan to come to his desk. The constable also followed him, closing the gate behind him.

I sat on that chair dejected. I couldn't believe that she had called the police. Was she ashamed of me? The questions kept haunting me the whole night. The inspector had assured Shubho and Armaan that he won't file a FIR against me, as it may spoil my future. It was an action in heat of moment and under the influence of alcohol. But since I didn't harm anyone physically, he was willing enough to give me another chance to act sober. But he warned that if next time something like that happens, he will definitely file a FIR. He wanted me to spend the night in the police station cell so that I could understand the severity of my actions.

In the morning a young boy brought me a cup of tea. He went around the police station to offer everyone a cup. Shubho and Armaan had also slept in the wooden bench placed by the wall of the inspector's room. The constable came and directed me to walk to the Inspectors' room. He was sitting behind his desk, wrapping up his duty hours. He looked up for a split second, before he went signing on a few documents in his desk. Once done, he walked towards me, sat by the corner of his table facing me. He said, "You are a bright young man and have a long career and life ahead. What you did yesterday night doesn't suit you. Learn to keep control on your emotions, and never repeat such actions again. I have not filed any report for you, but if you do anything similar or go near that apartment again for any nonsense, I will book you under various laws and spoil your life". He patted on my shoulders and said, "Now go home, get freshen up and move ahead in life. And while going take your two friends from the front office as well. You are lucky to have good friends".

Shubho went back to his home, and I went with Armaan. I was very quiet. The questions were still unanswered in my mind. Armaan preferred to leave me alone. Later in the day, I made him sit in front of me, "You were right. She was never mine. I was just smitten. I am seeing things more clearly now. I wanted to marry her. But actually marriage is the biggest sham of human society." He sat there with straight face hearing me out. "Marriage is just a rope to tie a lion, and the lion gets ready to get tied because he is made to think that he is getting old. Over the years it has become a race. The smart beautiful ones get married and send a SOS call to the world that we are taken. The normal ones who don't know what to do, look up to their parents to get them into a winning position of the race. For parents', marriage ceremony is just to show that their offspring are not left behind others. Forefathers thought that having kids outside marriage is not a good thing and not good for civil society, so they subscribed to the thought process of making marriage essential to have children and continue the family name. But nowadays married couples are having abortions and unmarried couples are getting children who instead are left in orphanages. Couples stay in live in without getting married, and married people stay as roommates. If you believe me, our next generation will definitely start losing trust on the institution of marriage. We are slowly drifting to the old animal world."

He stopped me with a motion of hand. His lips were parted and he was looking at me with surprise, "what has gone into you? What nonsense are you talking?"

"Its not nonsense. Its fact. I had drifted away from the truth. Female beauty always plays games with the male heart. And I also got into a game. But now I am in full control again."

"So what about Ankana?"

"What about her. She goes her way, I go mine"

"But weren't you in love with her till yesterday night"

"That's what I have been telling. You are not listening to me. Her beauty had trapped me, but now I am a free lion again. I am not going to stop at any girl now. I will live my independence again"

"so you mean to say that what you and Ankana had was not love, it was just a trap"

"Exactly"

"And who had set that trap?"

"The society, our mindset"

He folded his hands, "enough *Gyaan* today. Let's go out "

-- x --

Over the next few days, I transformed myself. I was putting more energy in office, and evenings it was with Armaan mainly. We tried to party hard, roam around, play games. We were trying to relive our college days again. On personal front, I was having full control on my emotions. I was feeling free. I had stopped calling her or even messaging her.

One evening we decided to go to Shubho's house to have special tea of Ruchi. I had not met them after the drunk incident. When we reached his apartment complex, the security guard stopped me. With an order of the society, I was barred from entering the complex. Security guard was a known guy to me, he said "Sir, after that day's incident, society has decided to not let you enter the complex till Ankana madam is living here"

I didn't protest or object. I just let Shubho know. Instead Ruchi brought her tea down and we had our tea standing outside on the pavement by the road. I deliberately didn't look up towards Ankana's balcony. I did want to, but I didn't. I was not sure how would I react if I see her. The past few days have been getting better and I wanted to keep it that way.

The Self Exploration

Akruti called me to inform that they are planning a get together party on her birthday. Past weeks I had been mostly with Armaan, and was not much in contact with either of Arpit-Neha, Piyush-Akruti or Shubho-Ruchi. I had deliberately been avoiding any meeting with the married couples. I used to talk to Arpit or Piyush on phone, but would avoid meeting with their better halves. Armaan had been telling me that everyone has observed my behavior, and no one approved of it.

So when Akruti called me instead of Piyush, I was very sure that I had to attend the party, and no excuses will be accepted. She did mention that she had invited friends from her professional life as well and her side of friends. So I did accept to be a part of her special day.

I dressed very professionally, in a blue suit with a grey shirt, and a pair of well-polished leather shoes. Akruti had once mentioned, she likes to cycle, but Piyush is not so willing. Hence she also didn't buy it. I thought it would be a great gift, so had already got it delivered to her home. That was my birthday gift for her. The party was in her building terrace. When I reached, the party was already in full swing. Bollywood numbers were playing in the background, a center makeshift dance floor had few couples dancing, men around the bar, and ladies sitting in a group formation on the other side. Food was kept on the far end, still covered with lids. Starters were kept by the side of the dance floor. It was a lavish party indeed. It was Akruti's first party post commitment and she wanted to make it grand. I believed she succeeded in her intentions.

As expected Armaan and Arpit were standing at the quietest corner drinking their beer. I walked to join them. Piyush came running and punched me hard on my shoulders. It was his way of saying Thank you for coming. Since being a couple, he had definitely sobered up a bit and gained a few kilos as well around his waist. He rushed back again to help Akruti. I had stopped drinking alcohol completely after I came back from Police Station. We were having normal chats when Arpit called out, "here comes Shubho" and we all turned towards the entrance. Shubho and Ruchi were followed closely by Ankana. As soon as they saw Ankana, they turned to see me. My lips were parted and my eyes like stone looking at that direction without a blink. I was standing motionless. A glimpse of her, brought back all our memories in an instant. The control on emotions I had been claiming for the past few days, was gone. I just wanted to run to her and fill her in my arms.

Arpit held me by my shoulder, and my chain of thoughts came to a sudden halt. Ankana had joined Ruchi and was standing with Akruti. Shubho walked to join us. Looking at my expression, he made his stand very clear "Akruti had invited Ankana as well, and since we were also coming this way, she came with us"

I took a few seconds to reply, "its okay *yaar*. Anyways I have stopped thinking about her. It doesn't matter to me anyhow". The fact being that I was struggling to stop myself from running towards her. But I tried to not make my thoughts obvious. Lately I had told everyone that I had no feelings for Ankana anymore. My ego was stopping me from accepting it otherwise, even in front of my best buddies.

The rest of the party I tried to act normal, but my eyes kept going back to her. It followed her like a spy. A couple of times she looked towards me, but her expression didn't change. It seemed she looked through me. My feelings were boiling within me. I wanted to go and talk to her, I was ready to do anything she wanted me to do.

At one instant when no one was watching, I gathered all my courage and walked towards her. She was standing with her back towards me. When I was just a couple steps away, Neha called her and she walked towards them. I could smell her scent in the air behind her. My love for her had never ended. I had tried hard to suppress the feelings within me. But it was very evident that a glimpse of her had made me weak in my knees.

I didn't know what to do. I rushed downstairs to the parking. To vent out my emotions I punched the pillar and cried out a loud howl. I was completely disturbed. Armaan and Arpit came running behind me. "I love her. Dammit, why doesn't she understand" I cried out loud

"Then why don't you go and tell her. She is upstairs" Arpit said

"I can't. I tried. I can't. I don't want to cry in front of her, but I feel I will not be able to control myself"

"Then don't. Just go and say it"

"No. There are so many guests upstairs. I don't want to ruin Akruti's party"

"Then what do you want to do?"

I punched the wall again "I wish I knew" I continued, "But how can she not feel anything for me, for our love. I know she loves me, but why is she still ignoring me. How is she able to control herself? Why she doesn't understand that Urmi tricked me. Why doesn't she understand I love her?"

"May be she needs some time"

Armaan said, "Let's go Daksh. Arpit you tell Akruti we left", and he held around my shoulders and walked me to his bike.

The whole night I sat in Armaan's balcony. I was lost in my thoughts. Around three in the morning, I messaged her, "You looked beautiful today. Couldn't gather courage to talk to you. I wish if we could"

I waited impatiently for the morning. I waited for her to wake up and reply to my message. But she didn't. I was getting desperate to talk to her. I just couldn't think, why I shouldn't talk to her. I tried calling her in the morning, but she didn't pick up my call. Again when I tried, she had switched off the phone. The instant thought that crossed my mind was that may be she was teaching a class in school and hence switched off her phone. I was surprised to find myself thinking in such optimistic way after so many days.

So I decided to go to her school and wait outside for her. After school may be I will talk to her. I waited in the bakery across the street, for the school to finish for the day. The kids came running out followed by the teachers. But I didn't find her. She didn't board her bus. In anxiety I walked towards the main gate of the school. To my surprise, I saw her leaving in a bike, sitting behind another male teacher. Anger took over me. How could she avoid me, forget me and get acquainted with another man in such a short duration.

I ran back to my bike which I had parked in front of the bakery. I rode behind their bike. I kept a safe distance for not to get noticed. She sat quietly behind him, sometimes bending forward to have a quick word with the man driving the bike. They took a path which was not leading to her home. This increased my anger. The previous day had ignited my love again. I felt possessive for her. I believed she was still mine, and only I had the right to drive her around.

They stopped by a saree shop. He waited outside on the bike, while she went inside. She came out quickly with a bag in her right hand. They again started and stopped by a known snacks shop. He parked the bike, and both went inside. I couldn't see them from outside, but I waited for them at some distance. They came out around twenty minutes later. Both were smiling and looked like they were having a great time in each other's company. He turned his bike and they drove to her home. She waved him a goodbye and went inside. I waited by the corner, and then I followed him and intercepted after a few kilometers in a residential colony with very minimal traffic.

He looked amused, but he stopped his bike. I parked my bike diagonally in front of his bike, stepped down and came towards him

"What happened? What do you want?" he asked me

"What's your name?'

"Why you want to know?"

"Just answer the questions" I tried acting tough

"But who are you?"

"I am someone whom you will remember for a long long time"

"Oh is it. Seems you are looking for trouble. May I know why, before I beat the hell out of you"

"Don't try acting smart just because you gave ride to a beautiful lady a few minutes back"

He took a moment, then his expression looked puzzled. "So you were following me?"

"Yes"

"But what do you want from me?" He asked

"I want you to get away from Ankana"

His puzzled look intensified, "So you know her. And you don't like her meeting me"

"Yes exactly"

"Either you are his brother or a big coward or a desperate man"

"You are free to think whatever you want" and I moved closer to him trying to instigate him. I was acting stupid and was ready for a dual with him.

He put the side stand of his bike and stepped down. He rolled over his shirt and walked towards me. In that instant I jumped and caught hold of his collar. He held my wrists. In my anger I was grinding my teeth "She is only mine. I love her. She is marrying me, and I don't want anyone to be around her" I spoke in a hushed voice with lot of intensity.

I could sense him ease of, his stiff shoulders gave way to a normal posture, and he asked "Are you Daksh?"

I looked surprised, "So she talks about me?"

He smiled, "Everyone in school talks about you." I looked even more astonished. He continued "And also about Urmi" and he smiled.

I let go of his collar, and turned around. I kicked my legs in air in frustration. "Why can't she understand that I didn't do anything wrong" I shouted in frustration. I turned back at him. My emotions were not constant. It was a mix of frustration, anger, optimism and feeling ridicule. Tears popped into my eyes, and I kneeled down feeling dejected. I held his legs and pleaded him "Please don't take her away from me. She is my life. I won't be able to live without her. She is not understanding. She is angry. One day when anger will subside, she will miss me. She will realize she is made only for me, and I am only for her. Please I beg, please don't take her away from me. Please" and I broke down crying.

He held my shoulders and helped me stand up. He tried to pacify me. He leaned me back on my bike, and gave his handkerchief to wipe my tears. It took me a while to calm myself. When he saw that I am getting a hold of myself, he walked back to his bike, wore his helmet and said "Take a break and pull back your life" and he zoomed off, while I sat there by the side of road depressed, crying and looking at a hollow incomplete future ahead.

While I was riding back, I received a call from Ankana. I stopped immediately by the side of road and took her call. In a very emotionless voice she spoke "Can we meet tomorrow evening?"

"We can meet now" I said

"Yes or No?"

"Definitely yes"

"Then meet me at Alfred's café at 5" and she hung up.

I couldn't believe that she called. I was too happy. I stayed awake whole night just waiting for the evening. I reached Alfred's café ten minutes earlier itself. I was dressed to my best. At exact five, Ankana walked in wearing a yellow and white saree, and a big purse in her arms. I was sitting in a table in middle of the room. She pointed towards the corner table and walked towards that. I followed behind. In a very emotionless voice she spoke "How are you?"

I wanted to say the truth, but with her just across the table, and the voice she spoke with, I replied "Am fine. What about you?"

She didn't respond to that. She instead said "Are you crazy?"

I looked back at her with wide eyes

"You have created so much fuzz about your broken heart. I never said a word and never reacted. But how could you confront my colleague? Will you let me live in this city or not. I could never have imagined your immaturity. You have been acting all teen. Am I a prize that you have to win? Was it that only your love was broken? You have made me a topic of discussion."

"But" I tried to interject with my defense

"Has it ever occurred to you that I could be scared? I left my family, my city to come and stay close to you. For me everything is new and everything is scary. Rather being my support, you have been just making my life difficult"

"But I have tried everything to get your attention, to talk to you, to give you my explanation. Yes I am crazy, as I have never been in love before, and for me you are what life is"

"Are you sure if this is love? Or is it just a fight to win me. You have always walked away from relationships, but no girl ever walked away from you. When I walked away from your home that day, did I open an ego struggle within you?"

"No no no. Why don't you understand that I love you?"

I didn't realize that I spoke in a bit louder voice and everyone was staring at us.

"I am sorry" I continued. "If you would have just spoken to me the first day itself, all these wouldn't have happened."

"How else would I have seen this side of yours?"

"You have seen the worst. I am better than that" I was trying desperately

"Every time I made up my mind and gathered the courage to come and talk with you, you had already created a mess. And with every mess my confidence in you reduced."

"But you also got me arrested" I snapped for a moment

She took a deep breath. "You made me an object that day whom everyone will talk forever. You were not listening to anyone. Who will say that you are an educated boy from a cultured family. Instead you were behaving like a road side Romeo. You didn't leave me an option."

"But how was getting me arrested a viable option. What if they would have beaten me up or spoilt my career. I didn't do anything intentionally. I was drunk."

"Why you were drunk like an alcoholic should be my question. But let me ask you, did the police file a report? Did they touch you with bad intent? No they didn't. Reason is that I pleaded to the inspector. Also I made sure to send your friends behind you."

I was shocked. I was angry. "You never gave me a chance to talk and now you are justifying your actions and intent"

She grabbed her purse, leaned forward "When you take an axe and hit a tree, there is a chance that tree wont fall at the first hit, but the axe leaves an everlasting impression on the trunk. Last couple of months has been that blow of axe on our relationship." She continued, "You have to come out clean, as a more matured person who can handle the ups and downs of a relationship. You have to do a lot of introspect and thinking. I want you to self-realize what all mistakes you did. And when you do that call me back. Take a few days off and be with yourself." She stood up and left the café.

I was quiet. Her words were heavy. They touched me deep within. A different kind of peace took over me. A peace of not having anything, a peace of not having the fear to lose anything more. The peace of an aloof leaf in the jungle. This kind of quietness is disruptive but essential. You have nowhere else to go, but a new path, a new beginning to start. All the baggage and the history you have been carrying to win something, is wiped off clean. The resilient energy to not accept defeat is taken over by the understanding of situation.

I went to the rest room, and put my head below running water. I don't remember how long I stayed there but it seemed eternal. I picked up my bike and drove to the lake. It was quiet and my inner self could talk loudly with me. I sat there till late in the night. I loved Ankana and could not love anyone like her. I knew she was my love of life, the one whom I really wanted to marry and spend my life, the one with whom I wanted to get old with. But lot of questions seemed to hover around that. Getting into another relationship was out of question, as I would never be able to love anyone with such intensity.

A part of me was getting depressed of not having her, but another part was pushing me to keep a strong face, to move on. I went home, quickly packed some basic cloths, took my camera, dropped a note to my manager for a week's leave, booked a self-drive car and left the city by early morning. I had no destination in mind. I just wanted time alone with me.

Shubho called me in the morning while I was driving through some broken village roads away from the city. I cut his call. But he was persistent. He kept calling. So I picked up his call. He was hysterical. He was standing in front of my door and there was no response to the doorbell. He had come upon to check on me. In a very calm dead voice, I said, "I am fine. Have left Bengaluru for a long drive. Will get back and call you. Don't worry I am fine, just need some time alone". He understood, but kept asking my location. I just hung up his call. A while later I stopped by a small tea shop. While sipping the extra sweet hot tea, I gave a call to Dad. I told him that I need some time and wanted to be away from phones, explanation, unnecessary talks for a few days. He asked if everything was fine. I didn't share much details and I think he too understood. Seems it's a man thing. I moved ahead on my drive.

Late in the evening, while I was driving through a narrow road somewhere deep in the territory, I realized that very less fuel was left in the car. The road was deserted, and till the horizon I couldn't see any light either of a house or any moving vehicle. There was no phone network available as well. I was really in middle of nowhere. There was no point of driving in the dark, till fuel ended. So I parked by the side of road, shifted to the back seat and slept. The feeling was as good as a night alone in a tent over a mountain top.

When the sun broke the darkness of night, I could see the beauty of the place I was in. It was lush green farms till the horizon, trees lining the intermittent boundaries created by human to segregate the piece of land which they claimed as their own. A mountain at the end was beaming happily in the first rays of morning. Birds were chirping and flying around. I couldn't resist and started capturing all these on my camera. Few minutes into my act, I saw the first trace of humanity. A bunch of kids dressed in light blue shirt and dark blue pants were riding their cycle towards school. I stopped them. They didn't understand Hindi, but could understand a few

English words. Anyways, I asked them about the nearest highway and the town. Within their giggles and local language talk, I could pick a few keywords for my purpose. I could get a very vague idea of the directions.

So I started again and after a few kilometers, joined a highway. I stopped at the first food dhaba by the road for breakfast. A few trucks were standing there as well, who had halted after a night's drive. I ordered aloo parathas and lassi and settled down with my phone. After a night of peace, my phone finally had a network. There were four missed calls from Ankana and a message – "If possible please call back"

So I called her back "Hi, tell me"

"Nothing. Just wanted to make sure you are okay"

"Yes I am fine."

"I heard you went on a long drive. So where are you?"

I confirmed with the truckers near me, and responded "somewhere near Agumbe"

"Wow. You drove quiet far."

"Yes, didn't realize"

"So when are you planning to be back?"

"A few days may be"

"Okay. Enjoy your trip. Take lot of pictures and do share some"

"Sure."

"Bye" and she hung up

I had a smile on my face. It felt good talking to her. After a long time, I was feeling light. I was feeling me. I had my breakfast over nice conversations with the truck drivers. They had many stories to share. A good few hours later, I was back on road. I filled up gas and headed towards the Arabian Sea.

Over the next few days I crisscrossed the Konkan area, jog falls, numerous villages and small towns, lot of temples. I met lot of people and lot of photography. It felt good. It felt liberating. I could breathe oxygen. I kept my family and friends informed with some messages and pictures. I planned to drive down to Mangalore and then back to Bengaluru.

Armaan came up with a plan to meet at Coorg. He planned to come down in a bus so that he could accompany me back to Bengaluru. I was happy to halt at Coorg waiting for my friend. I waited for him outside the Madikeri bus stand. I could see Armaan de-boarding the bus, followed by Piyush, Arpit and Shubho. My whole gang was there. I ran towards them for a hug. It was a very emotional moment. A loud horn by a passing bus brought us back to senses.

Armaan had booked a cottage within the hills and we drove while he navigated. It was after so many years that we all were together. Once in cottage, we all freshened up. I had been continuously on road and not had a proper bath since I left Bengaluru. The bath was rejuvenating but I didn't shave. We settled down in the lawn after food. We had so much to discuss. We didn't roam around but preferred to stay at room. We ordered drinks in the evening as it was getting a bit cold. The discussions also shifted from leg pulling to intellectual ones.

"No one had thought we all will change so much" said Piyush

"What changes are you talking about?" asked Arpit.

"The changes after ladies have come in our lives" Piyush said

We looked at Armaan, "He will never change" said Shubho

"Why so confident?" asked Armaan

"Because you won't ever get one"

"If Piyush can get a girl, even I can. It's just a matter of time" Armaan protested.

"Yes man we have changed" said Arpit while looking towards the ceiling

"Who would have thought that Piyush will settle down so early? That Shubho will turn out to be an uncle so early. That Arpit can be tamed by just a look. That Daksh will become over involved in a relationship" said Armaan.

They all looked at me. I was sitting quietly by the corner of the bed enjoying the conversation and my drink. "What?" I asked

"You have to tell" said Arpit

"Nothing man. I feel so idiot thinking about the past few months. The last few days have brought so much clarity. I was immature in my relationships earlier. I was in an extreme. An extreme of non-committal. You all thought I was stud, but frankly I was stupid. I could have been a better man. But then because of multiple factors I planned to get married, get settled. Parents were pushing, you all were getting settled and looking at you all I felt commitment was not that scary. And while I was entering that phase, I met Ankana. She seemed perfect. She has beauty, poise, good balance of tradition and modern, and above all she made me feel complete. I got myself over committed. I switched from one extreme to another. I started feeling we were married and that we had one unique identity. I developed high expectations. But what I missed to understand was that she has self-identity apart from the relationship. I missed to understand that she had her fears, her thoughts, and her inhibitions. I tried to push my position in her life, assuming that I have already cemented that position. I was such a lost cause. Frankly speaking I am myself ashamed of Daksh for his actions over last few months. I always had the habit of ending relationships because frankly I was commitment phobic. But when finally I got involved in seriousness with someone, I could feel the actual pain of love when she walked off. It hurts. The feeling of losing someone is unbearable." I said in a very deep voice but in a calm composed way.

"So now what?" asked Shubho

"I don't have a plan. I have a job, I have my hobbies, I have you all and I have a girl I wish who can give me another chance"

We cheered up our glasses, "to the ladies of our lives"

The talks continued till late night. Morning we woke up, and planned to do some tourist site visits before heading back to Bengaluru.

By the time we entered Bengaluru, it was late evening. Akruti invited us all for dinner. So we drove to Piyush's home. Ruchi, Neha and Ankana were already there helping Akruti with the cooking. As soon as we entered Akruti rushed to give Piyush a kiss, Ruchi and Shubho wrapped arms around each other, while Neha pulled Arpit to a corner for a quick chat. Ankana looked at me, but as soon as our eyes met, I looked down. Armaan had reached kitchen in search of something to nibble.

I was not expecting Ankana there. I didn't know how to react or what to say. I felt shy. I gathered my strength and gave a sheepish smile to Ankana. She walked near me, and led me towards the open balcony. We stood there silently looking at the road and vehicles at a distance.

"So how was the trip?" she asked

"Quite liberating" I responded

"The pictures you shared were quite good. You are a good photographer"

"Yes the places were good"

"Next time I will also come with you"

"And the experience was great" I completely missed her statement. It took me a few seconds to realize what she said. So I continued "Will you come along?". Within me I just wanted to hear affirmative.

"Sure if you take me along"

"Why would I not take you?"

"You may have your own reasons"

I just smiled back. She continued "But I have a condition"

With big anxious eyes I looked back at her, "We will leave your beard behind" and she had a big laugh.

I looked at her with admiration. I saw the Ankana which I missed the most. I so wanted to fill her in my arms.

"What" she asked as I stood there with a smile

"Nothing. I don't know what to say"

She spoke after a few moments of silence "Let's make a fresh start" and she slipped her hands in mine. We stood there in the balcony facing the city. The city looked much beautiful now.

Behind us everyone stood there giving each other a Hi-Five.

Printed in Great Britain
by Amazon